PERFECTLY HONEST

LINDA O'CONNOR

Best wishes, Kim!
Linda

SOUL MATE PUBLISHING
New York

PERFECTLY HONEST

LINDA O'CONNOR

Cover Design by Rae Monet, Inc.

Published in the United States of America by
Soul Mate Publishing
P.O. Box 24
Macedon, New York, 14502

ISBN: 978-1-61935-737-2
eBook ISBN: 978-1-61935-672-6

www.SoulMatePublishing.com

This book is dedicated to:

Lesley Rooke — for always making the positive voice the loudest.

My men — my life is better with you. I love you.

Acknowledgements

I would like to thank Debby Gilbert at Soul Mate Publishing for providing the ultimate encouragement to my writing with the leap to publishing. Huge thanks to the team at Soul Mate Publishing including Rae Monet for the beautiful cover design and editor Janine Phillips.

It's an amazing feeling when your children grow up and teach you.
Brad, who has shown me that changing course can open doors and be its own reward;
Tom, who has humbled me with his example of perseverance, his willingness to put himself in a position to succeed, his thoughtfulness and kindness;
Mark, who inspires me with his imagination;
I love you and am so very proud to be your mom.

Thank you from my heart to:
Vlad, who promoted my writing before I had the courage,
my mom, who gardens so I can write,
Karen, who shares her coloring and Paul, his photography,
Cathy and Ellie for their eagle eyes, and the 'Ladies of the Book Club,' who join me in my love of reading.

I've had so much fun writing — I hope it shines through in the words and passes along to you, the reader, as a thank you for choosing to read my book.

Chapter 1

Written in the Stars by Esmeralda Garnet

ARIES (March 21-April 19) Life will be hectic and not much will go as planned. Revisiting an old hobby or trying something new should be your goal. Nurture the relationships that mean the most to you.

Dr. Mikaela Finn sat back and rolled her shoulders. One more chart and she'd be done. Finally. What a day. Between the delivery at two in the morning, the emergency C-section, her morning clinic of complicated prenatal patients, and an afternoon clinic that never seemed to end, she was toast.

She blew out a breath and looked up at the sign on her door. Dr. Mikaela Finn. Obstetrician and Gynecologist. It still gave her a thrill to read it. She laughed at herself. After six months she should be used to it, but it had been a long road. Finishing and passing her exams had been exciting enough, but being offered a junior position at St. Peter's where she'd trained had been icing on the cake. Clinic space, operating time, and an office within running distance to the delivery suite had been quite the coup.

Or so she had thought.

It was absolutely crazy. Rivermede was a good-sized city with a population of about one hundred thousand. But add in the catchment area of surrounding small towns with very fertile people, and it meant non-stop work. Plus, it didn't help that the senior staff and half the nurses still saw her as a trainee. Saying 'no,' to the endless stream of requests was hardly an option.

But something had to give. She had considered change and had sent out a couple of letters to hospitals in other towns, thinking change would be good, challenging even.

Just one problem.

She feared change.

So unless she found time to research and plan, she'd be staying put. In the meantime, a little practice saying 'no' in the mirror might be a good idea.

She clicked on the patient chart and started typing. Her brain felt slow. She had kept a very satisfying caffeine buzz going all day with three coffees and a chocolate bar, but it had worn off when the last patient walked out the door. Focus. Shit, what had she told that mom? Sex? No sex? Sex on Sundays? She envied the era of hand written charts. Write a few illegible squiggles and be done.

She finished the note, shut down her computer, and gave a huge yawn. Food or sleep? The thought of soft pillows and a warm comforter had her sighing. Food could wait.

Her cell phone rang as she shrugged on her coat. She checked the call display, half-afraid to see the hospital switchboard. Margo, she read with a smile.

"Mikaela, I have a favor to ask."

That was enough to send a shot of adrenalin through her. She could count on one hand the number of times her best friend had asked for a favor in the past ten years. "Of course. Ask away."

Margo hesitated. "I shouldn't even bother you with this, but I'm in such a bind."

Mikaela heard the uncertainty and worry. "What? Do you need a kidney? Bone marrow? You're killing me. What is it?"

Margo laughed. "Sorry, you're right. Nothing so drastic. Although I need your time, which is probably a hotter commodity than your kidney," Margo said with a sigh. "For the past two weeks, Chloe and I have been painting a house for a client. I flew to Rainy River for a meeting this morning and left Chloe to finish the last room. Which she should have been able to do. Except, this morning she slipped and broke her wrist."

"Oh no. Poor Chloe. Is she okay?"

"Yes, she's fine. She went to the Emergency Department. She's in a cast for six weeks and pretty high on painkillers, but at least she didn't need surgery. Luckily Rip's home and can help with the triplets. The problem is, I can't get a flight home until tomorrow morning. I promised the client I would have the painting done and everything put back by tomorrow, but Chloe said the bedroom still needs another coat of paint."

"So you need me to go over and finish it?" Mikaela asked.

Margo sighed. "Yes. I know you haven't painted in a few years now, but . . . yes."

"Why don't you just explain to the client what happened and ask if it would be okay to take another day?"

"We were already cutting it pretty close. Tomorrow night there's a big party planned. They want to showcase the entire house because it's going on the market. The event planner will be there at noon."

"Jeez."

"I know. I'm really sorry to ask."

"No. No. Not at all. Of course I can do it." It brought back memories of all the summers they spent painting to earn money for school. Mikaela had gone on to do a residency. Margo kept the business running. "What's the address?"

"1273 Pinewood."

"No problem. I'll grab a bite to eat and head over."

"I'll text you the code for the front door. If you have any problems, just call me. Chloe said she got the first coat on, so if you could get the painting done, that would be fantastic. Leave the cleaning. I can get there first thing in the morning and do the rest. Mikaela, thank you so much."

Mikaela dragged herself to her car and, with a detour to Tim Horton's for an extra large coffee, drove home. With a look of longing at her bed, she grabbed a change of clothes and headed over to 1273 Pinewood.

Mikaela stepped back and eyed her work. The third coat of paint had done the trick. The streaks and faint trace of the original color had finally disappeared, leaving a velvety smooth finish. She tossed the brush with the other rollers, trays, and paint cans that were strewn all over the drop cloth protecting the floor.

Even covered in a tarp, the oversized chair in the middle of the bedroom looked too tempting. She really shouldn't relax now. She should finish up and go.

She eyed the chair.

Just five minutes.

Mikaela sank down into the softness of goose down feathers, threw her head back, and closed her eyes. It was like floating on a cloud.

She had done a delivery, a C-section, two full clinics, and three hours of painting, all on four hours of sleep. Her arms and shoulders ached from the exercise. Stray soft brown hair escaped her ponytail, brushed her face, and tickled her nose. She didn't even have the energy to raise her arm and brush it away.

So far Esmeralda's horoscope had been bang on. Hectic – no surprise there - and a change in plans. Change. When she read that, she almost flipped to Zodiac Zach. She had apps for three astrologers and picked the one she liked best. She wasn't sure if she really believed in them, but it was surprising how often they were right. Like today. Turned out, it wasn't so bad. She could handle change if it meant helping Margo.

Mikaela opened one eye and glanced at her watch. Midnight. She really should get up, clean the paintbrushes, and go home. Then crawl into bed and sleep for, well, she groaned, six hours. If she was lucky.

Just five minutes.

As every muscle in her body relaxed, Mikaela smiled to herself and wondered what the homeowner would think if he knew he had the highest paid painter in the city.

Mikaela woke with a start to the sound of voices. Disoriented, in unfamiliar surroundings, she looked down at her short shorts and loose shirt covered with spatters of paint. Painting, of course. She must have fallen asleep in the chair, and checking her watch, she saw that it was two o'clock in the morning. Shit. She rubbed her eyes and yawned. Pulling herself out of the chair, she listened to the voices. One voice was female, sounding impatient and unhappy and one male, sounding apologetic and resigned.

"I know it's not ideal, Sophia, but it's what I want. I'm tired of the large city, the tertiary care center, and all the politics. I'm tired of all the meetings and all the committees. I want a smaller hospital in a smaller city. I want a life."

"Nonsense, Sam," the woman shot back. "You don't know what you want or what's good for you. You need to pay your dues now to reap the benefits later."

"Look, I don't expect you to understand. I'm grateful you've agreed to help me out, but . . . "

Mikaela wandered into the hallway and stopped when she saw the two of them at the front door. The woman had unbuttoned her coat, and as she put her hands on her hips, there was a flash of the red cocktail dress she wore underneath. The man was a foot taller and wearing a suit. A very nice fitting suit, Mikaela mused, as she came up behind him.

The woman noticed Mikaela first, and her startled gasp had the man looking over his shoulder. Mikaela wasn't sure who looked more shocked, the man, who moved to shield the woman, or the woman, who raked her gaze over Mikaela from head to toe. As Mikaela fought the urge to straighten her shirt and fix her hair, she decided, definitely, the woman.

The woman's eyes narrowed, the hands on her hips became clenched at her sides, and her face flushed red. Mikaela held her breath.

The woman pushed at the man's shoulder and spun him around to face her. "Why you! You! 'I can't invite you in, the house is being painted,'" she mimicked. "Is that the new code word for 'mistress?' You could have just told me we were through. Well, I'm done. This is the last straw. You pig!" The woman spun on her heel and wrenched the door open.

"Sophia, wait!"

"No, wait," Mikaela added. She lurched forward, now wide-awake.

The woman stormed out and slammed the door.

The man turned to Mikaela. "Who the hell are you?"

Chapter 2

Zodiac Zach – Don't leave home without him.

ARIES (March 21-April 19) Consider your options so that you can balance your personal and professional life. Use your heart and intuition as your guide.

"Mikaela Finn. I am so sorry. I came over tonight to finish the painting and I fell asleep in your chair. Great chair, by the way." She cleared her throat. "I wasn't expecting you to come home. I'm very sorry," she said, looking anxiously at the closed door. "I feel terrible. Would you like me to try to catch her and straighten this out?"

"I don't think it will help. Shit." He raked his hand through his hair. "I needed her."

Mikaela's eyebrows winged up. Really? He was tall, and wavy dark hair skimmed the collar of his finely tailored suit, making the open buttons, loose tie, and slightly rumpled shirt look out of place. This gorgeous hunk of a man 'needed' that woman? For what? She didn't seem to respect him or trust him. Jeez, she didn't even wait for an explanation. Must be good in bed, Mikaela thought, and smirked.

He looked at her and crossed his arms. "Sophia promised to help me out. You think you could do a better job?"

"Probably."

"Fine, let's just see." He took a step closer.

"Just a minute, buster." Mikaela stumbled back.

"I have a job interview in Emerson this weekend. It's the last round of hoops I have to jump through for a new job. And I really want this job. It's a small town and they've hinted they would rather hire someone who's married and willing to settle there. So I'm bringing my fiancée to meet them. That would be you."

"What?"

"Sophia agreed to play the part of my fiancée, and I don't have time to find someone else."

"I can't do that. I don't even know you."

"I'm Sam O'Brien. What do you need to know? You just said you could do a better job. What did you think I was talking about?"

Mikaela thought about having sex and cleared her throat. "Ironing your shirts," she said instead.

Sam smiled and took a step closer. She put her hand out against his chest to stop him. Her heart stuttered at the interest that flared in his eyes and the firm muscle under her hand.

"I've been ironing my own shirts for a long time. I don't need help with that," he drawled.

"Really? Looks like I could teach you a few things about adding heat and steam. You know, it works better when things are wet." Mikaela stood absolutely still. Where had that come from?

Sam chuckled and sent her an appreciative glance. "And here I thought smooth gliding back and forth with the right amount of pressure is all that's needed." His voice was deep and smooth.

She swallowed. He was hot and the image *that* created sent shivers all the way to her toes. She was playing with fire. It was late, and she was a little punch drunk from fatigue. It was time to go. She took a step back.

Sam put his hands in his pockets. "So you'll do it? You'll come with me this weekend?"

"Why me? I can't imagine you having trouble finding a woman."

"I'm so flattered." He grinned. "I've tried. Sophia wasn't the first. Apparently the whole concept of a 'fake' fiancée is hard to grasp. Fake. As in one weekend only. I need someone with no emotional attachment. It's just a weekend."

"So you're saying I'm your last choice."

Sam raked his eyes down the length of her. "Oh no. You're my top pick right now."

She knew he was joking but couldn't stop the swirl in her chest. Those gorgeous blue eyes looked pretty serious.

"It's two days away. I'd really appreciate your help," Sam said, looking at her hopefully.

Mikaela eyed Sam. Should she do it? He looked sincere. It was kind of her fault that Sophia had stormed out. Then again, the woman didn't seem very nice, maybe she did him a favor. She would love to get away. Out of town meant out of reach and no work. That sounded heavenly. And Zodiac Zach did say to balance work and play. She looked at Sam with his devilish good looks. Did she dare?

Sam raised his brows at her.

"Maybe."

Sam let out a breath. "Great. I'll take that as a yes."

"Yes, well, I'm not saying I'll do any . . . ironing. Let's just be clear on that."

"Sure, no ironing. Got it." He grinned. "I'll pick you up on Saturday morning. Bring an overnight case. There's a dinner on Saturday night and a brunch on Sunday morning. We'll be back by Sunday evening. I really do appreciate this and I promise, you won't regret it."

Chapter 3

happenstance horoscope

ARIES (March 21-April 19) Don't let uncertainty lead to disappointment. Be prepared and follow through with your plans. Taking a risk will help you achieve more than you thought possible.

What the hell was she thinking? Two nights sleep and time to ruminate left her wondering why she had ever agreed.

Okay, she knew his name. Sam O'Brien. He was six foot two, looked great in Armani suits, and ironed his own shirts. She winced at the memory of that conversation.

Needing more, Mikaela had done some investigating. She called Margo and asked her what she knew. Which hadn't been much. Google and Facebook weren't very helpful. She could contact her dad and he'd check Sam out and give her all the information she needed. He wouldn't mind, in fact, he'd prefer it. But she didn't really want to go there. In the end, she did the next best thing and called Jack, her father's head of security. It was a little scary how much information was out there, if you knew what you were doing.

So. Sam O'Brien. Healthy, financially secure, three credit cards, one line of credit, no major debts, owned property in Rivermede and in Emerson, no police record, not in the FBI or Interpol database, and had three outstanding parking tickets. Jack said to go ahead and date him.

Mikaela took a deep breath. She hadn't mentioned she was going to spend the weekend with him.

Next problem?

She had no idea what to wear.

Mikaela looked around her bedroom at the mess. Her normally tidy room was littered with various combinations of leggings, long sweaters, skinny jeans, lacy tops, scarves, and a cropped jacket. She loved clothes, but putting together an outfit was crazy. There was the weather to consider, the activity, her mood that day. By the time she factored in all the variables, she was ready to throw in the towel and wear a paper bag.

And the footwear decisions. Flats, stylish ankle boots, fashion forward thigh-high boots, casual sneakers, and heels. It was all too much.

She glanced out the window and focused on the soothing sound of the waves gently lapping the shore. She had been living in a condominium on the shore of Lake Ontario for the past two years and never tired of watching the changing pattern of the lake. Whether it was smooth as glass in the winter, slow and steady in a light breeze of the summer, or crashing wildly in the high winds of the fall, it never failed to calm her and help her keep things in perspective.

She needed a little fun and wanted a little adventure. And didn't that happenstance horoscope agree? She needed to stop worrying. But maybe she should stick with flats over heels, just in case.

Finally, dressed in skinny jeans, a pale blue lace top and a cream scarf, Mikaela finished the rest of her packing. She hung up the clothes she chose not to bring, debating again whether she might need them and then, with a shake of her head, put them away. Everything was hung or stacked neatly in the walk-in closet.

Mikaela checked the time. Twenty minutes to spare.

She carried her case downstairs, set it by the front door and wandered into the living room. She had recently painted over the builder's beige with a warm buttery yellow. It reminded her of a sandy beach on a sunny day. A pale blue-gray sofa and two small armchairs in white surrounded a frosted blue glass coffee table. A stunning watercolor, painted by Margo as a housewarming gift, hung above the sofa and pulled all the colors together. The sunlight streaming in the huge picture window added to the ambiance of a relaxing seaside beach house.

When the doorbell rang, Mikaela took one last deep breath and opened the door.

Sam was dressed casually in jeans and a short-sleeved black shirt, showing off a broad chest and muscular arms. "Hi. You look lovely this morning." He greeted her with a smile. "More rested."

Mikaela smiled ruefully. "Thanks. Come in."

As Sam stepped in, his cell phone rang. He checked the caller ID and looked at Mikaela apologetically. "Sorry, it's the hospital. I should answer." He turned his back slightly. "Dr. O'Brien."

Dr. O'Brien? Sam's a doctor? Jack didn't mention that. Maybe he thought she already knew. She looked at Sam closely, wondering if she'd seen him at the hospital. And then it hit her. Dr. Sam O'Brien. The ophthalmologist? The one they called Dr. Eye Candy? She hadn't met him, but had heard about him from the operating room nurses. He was a playboy, but interestingly, they had a lot of good things to say about him, despite his reputation of lovin' and leavin' 'em. Apparently, he was just as good at loving as he was at leaving. He left the door open a crack, and they hoped he would walk through again. That may be, but she certainly had no intention of becoming part of his gaggle of female followers or being another notch in his bedpost. Forewarned was forearmed.

"Sure, put him through," Sam said into the phone. "Hi, Nick, what's up?" After a few minutes of listening, Sam started asking questions to clarify the history he was obviously hearing about. "What's his vision? And that's documented? When did the accident happen? He'll need an enucleation. I'm heading out of town until tomorrow, but send him to the General and admit him. Get the CT scan results, too. I have OR time on Monday and could operate then." He paused and listened. "Fine, I'll see him tomorrow night. Sure. No problem. Bye." Sam sighed as he disconnected. He turned back to Mikaela. "Sorry about that."

"No problem," Mikaela said. "So, you're a doctor?"

Sam tilted his head. "Yes, I'm an ophthalmologist, an eye surgeon. Problem?"

"No," Mikaela said hastily. "I overheard your conversation. Are you on call?"

"No, I'm not, but I've had extra training in orbital problems, so I always get called for those."

"I see." Ophthalmology, she thought. That explained why she hadn't seen him around. She worked at St. Peter's Hospital, the ophthalmology department was at Rivermede General.

"Don't worry," he said. "You're in good hands. If anything happens, I can check your vision."

Mikaela laughed.

He picked up her bag and turned toward the door. "Ready to go?"

Chapter 4

Written in the Stars by Esmeralda Garnet

ARIES (March 21-April 19) Visiting unfamiliar places or meeting new acquaintances will influence the direction you want to take. Focus on helping others. Romance is highlighted.

Mikaela sat back comfortably in the low-slung seat of a sexy black Jaguar and enjoyed the power and speed as they chewed up the miles. "So tell me more about why we're doing this."

Sam glanced over. "I needed a change."

Wow, someone who actually sought change, Mikaela mused. She couldn't relate. "Tired of ophthalmology?"

"No, I like ophthalmology. It's all the rest I could live without. The meetings, research, teaching." He paused for a moment. "It's sort of like being a hockey player and being asked to play defense, right wing and goalie. I'd like to be able to pick one and stick with it."

"And that one would be patient care?"

"Yes, exactly."

"How would Emerson be better?"

"No teaching, less research, fewer meetings. And more operating room time."

"Perfect combo," she agreed. "What's with all the schmoozing? Why don't you just hang up your shingle and start to work?"

Sam laughed. "Seems like you should be able to. But I need hospital privileges. If I can't operate, I don't want to make the move. And *that* is up to the board of directors. Emerson's a small community, and they want to make sure new staff fit in."

"And a woman in your life makes you a better person?"

"Always," Sam said with a smile. Her heart stuttered. "I want them to know I'm serious about staying. Apparently a single guy doesn't fit that profile. It's not written in stone," Sam said as he glanced over to her, "but it's come up. A lot. The hospital is underserviced for a number of specialties. Part of this weekend will be trying to convince them that ophthalmology is a priority."

"The patients would be lucky to have an ophthalmologist in town."

"Hopefully, they'll see it that way too," he said, with a grin. "I have to go and present rounds at one o'clock this afternoon. I'm meeting some of the family doctors and giving a talk about common eye problems. I expect it will take a couple of hours. I can drop you off, and you can get a bite to eat and relax. Dinner starts at seven, and we'll meet the rest of the board, about thirty people in all. Not shy, I hope?"

Not any more, she thought. Medical school had cured her of that pretty quickly. "Nope, I'll be fine," she replied. "Where are we staying?"

"Here," he said, exiting the highway onto a tree-lined street. After a short distance, he drove down a narrow gravel road, where low branches brushed the car, and then turned onto a long paved lane.

"We're not staying in Emerson?"

Sam shook his head. "I have a cottage here. Last year I had some major renovations done, so I can stay here year round." He glanced over at her. "Is that okay?"

"I thought I would get a chance to look around Emerson if we were staying in town," she lied.

"If you want to head into town, it's not a problem. Just go back out to the main highway and continue for another five kilometers. I keep another vehicle here, a Jeep. So if you want to venture into town, feel free," he reassured her. "I thought this would be easier for sleeping arrangements," he admitted without looking at her. "There's lots of space, and you can have your own bedroom. With no questions asked. It's a small town." He glanced over at her. "Unless you've changed your mind about that?" he asked with a smile.

"No, that sounds perfect," she quickly agreed.

As they rounded the next bend in the drive, the view opened up to a clearing. Mikaela caught her breath at the beauty.

She expected a little cottage in the backwoods of the lot, like a rugged man-cave.

This was not that.

This was a beautiful, stunning piece of art, made of glass and stone, which melded with the environment. She stared at the asymmetry of the roofline and the staggered design of the building as it curved around a majestic maple tree. The image of a sexy lady lying on her side and winking as she invited you in popped into Mikaela's head. Even the tree's canopy looked like an elegant fan keeping the mistress cool, as it swayed in the light breeze. She laughed at the fanciful thought.

Mikaela looked over at Sam with delight. "This is amazing," she said. "It's so beautiful."

Sam looked over at the house, obviously pleased. "Thanks. My brother's an architect and when I bought this property, he was excited about designing the house. He was like a kid in a candy store, testing all kinds of new things. It was fun to work with him."

"Well, the result is spectacular. It looks modern and rustic at the same time. Like it's part of the environment."

Sam nodded. "That was the idea," he said. "Come on. I'll show you inside."

He parked the car and grabbed their bags from the back. He led her down the walkway, which curved around the maple tree, to the front door, a plain slab of rich chocolate brown wood. Sam flipped open a small compartment hidden in the frame and pressed his right index finger to the panel. The door slid open.

"Here," he said. "Give me your hand and I'll code you in, so you can come and go."

He pressed a series of numbers and then, drawing her close to him, he took her hand gently in his and pressed her index finger to the scanner. Mikaela caught her breath at the brief, gentle contact. She was acutely aware of the firmness of his chest against her back and his warm, earthy smell.

"There you go," he said quietly. "Just press your finger to the scanner and the door will unlock or lock behind you if you're leaving."

Mikaela cleared her throat as she stepped away from him. "Thanks. Good to know."

He picked up the bags again, and nodded for her to go inside.

Mikaela slipped off her shoes in the foyer and walked to the left, into a sitting area. High ceilings soared above a sleek stone fireplace, filling one wall. Floor to ceiling windows across the back wall, interrupted by glass French doors, allowed a breathtaking view of a lake in the back.

"Oh, you're on the water here," she said, smiling at Sam.

"Yes, it's not a very big lake, but enough for kayaking in the summer and skating in the winter."

"It's really lovely, Sam."

"I'll show you around."

They walked to the right, behind the foyer into the kitchen. It was white and gray, with an expanse of veined marble on the countertops and island. A gray and white marble backsplash in smaller tiles set off elegant gray cabinets. A circular white table sat in a little nook overlooking the lake.

"It all looks brand new," Mikaela exclaimed.

Sam laughed. "Someone comes to help with the cleaning and upkeep through the week, when I can't get here. And, lucky for me, she loves to cook. She keeps the fridge well stocked with homemade meals and fresh produce, mostly from her garden, I think. So," he grinned, "the kitchen doesn't get a lot of use. I like to think I'm saving her some work by not messing it up."

"That's very considerate of you," Mikaela said, with a grin.

They continued through the kitchen into a larger, formal dining area. An entertainment room filled with a large-screen television, comfy recliners, and a large sofa branched off to the front of the house. Toward the back of the house, another room housed fitness equipment. And finally, down a short hallway, Sam stopped in front of a bedroom adjacent to a study.

"You can use this room," Sam said as he set down her bag. "My room is down at the end of the hall. The bathroom is through here." He showed her a door that connected the guest room and the study to a shared bath.

An inviting Jacuzzi filled the corner, and a glass shower complete with body jets and a rain head was opposite the tub. *Oh, there's even a towel warming rack.* She sighed, thinking she may never leave.

Sam checked his watch. "Look, I should get going. Make yourself at home. Help yourself to anything in the fridge. I should be home by four o'clock at the latest. Anything else before I head out?"

She shook her head. "No. I'll get something to eat and sit outside by the water and read. I brought a book, and I'll enjoy the quiet. Thank you."

Sam smiled. "Thank you for doing this. I really appreciate it. When I get back, we can sit down and get our story straight."

"Sounds good. Don't worry about me. I'll be fine," she said, stepping toward her bag sitting in the middle of her room.

Sam strode down the hall to his bedroom and closed the door behind him with a soft click.

Mikaela unpacked her things, and then with her stomach growling, she headed to the kitchen for food. As she pulled a shrimp salad out of the fridge, Sam came through the kitchen.

He had changed into a dark suit, crisp white shirt and tie. *God, he was gorgeous.* Broad shoulders, flat stomach, slim hips, muscular thighs. Blue eyes and wavy, thick dark hair. A devilish smile. Charming and considerate. And he smelled . . . delicious. A wave of sheer lust shot through Mikaela as she stared at him. She could hear him saying something to her, something about keys and the Jeep, but images of her and Sam, naked together, crowded out any other coherent thought.

"Okay?" Sam asked, looking at her with a puzzled expression.

"Huh? Yeah," she stammered. She forced a smile. "Great, thanks."

Sam turned to leave. Mikaela had no idea what he'd just said, and with a wince, hoped it wasn't important.

Focus, she told herself. It's Sam O'Brien, Dr. Eye Candy. Stay away. Stay far, far away.

She did not want to be his statistic or one of his many. And the last thing she needed was to provide fuel for the hospital rumor mill. She watched him walk away with catlike grace, admiring his ass and the fine picture he made in a suit. She groaned. Food, she thought. Was sugar an antidote for raging hormones? She hoped so.

Chapter 5

Zodiac Zach – Don't leave home without him.

ARIES (March 21-April 19) Physical activity will alleviate stress. Offering your skills in unusual ways will open new opportunities. You have more to offer than you realize.

An hour later, Mikaela was reclining sleepily on a deck chair out back by the lake. She had enjoyed a delicious shrimp salad and fresh bread. She found the most decadent homemade chocolate chunk cookies (thank you person who does the cleaning and shopping) and enjoyed two, well four, if you counted the ones she had eaten standing up. Which technically, she knew, did not count.

When she came out to the backyard, she was stunned to see a full-sized tennis court and a glass addition, housing a swimming pool. The light glinted off the domed roof and glass panels, and the water shimmered invitingly inside. An indoor swimming pool. Was anything more luxurious? She loved to swim. In the summer, she was in the lake every day, and in the winter made a point of going to the local pool two or three times a week. She eyed the pool and wondered if Sam would mind if she went for a swim.

Mikaela pushed herself up and wandered over. She tried the handle of the glass-paneled door, but it was locked. Oh, too bad. It looked like a beautiful pool. There were tropical plants and more reclining chairs inside. A stack of beach towels sat near a slate bar. Shades were drawn around some of the walls, maybe another experiment in technology?

Turning to go, she spied a box on the doorframe like the one at the front door. She flipped open the lid and with only a slight hesitation, pressed her index finger to the scanner. The doors slid silently open.

That was cool. Mikaela wandered in, admiring the pristine condition and elegant stone surrounding the pool. Dipping her hand in the water, she sighed with pleasure at the soft warmth.

Mikaela stood at the edge of the pool weighing her options. She didn't have a swimsuit. She looked outside at the forest surrounding the pool house. Not a neighbor in sight. She hadn't heard or seen another soul in the past hour. It was only two o'clock and Sam wasn't expected back for another two hours. What would be the harm of a quick dip? A few lengths, half an hour tops. It looked so inviting. She would feel refreshed and could burn off some of the sexual energy shimmering through her.

Enough good reasons, Mikaela thought, and with one more glance around, stripped. Folding her clothes and leaving them on one of the chairs, she went to the stairs and waded in.

Mikaela sighed with pleasure as the warm water brushed her skin. She couldn't recall skinny-dipping, ever, but decided she should definitely do it more often. Diving underwater, she enjoyed the silky brush of water against her breasts without the encumbrance of a swimsuit. She swam the length of the pool and with a flip and a push off the wall, eased into the rhythm of doing lengths. Eight strokes, flip and push.

Mikaela continued with the easy rhythm until her arms and legs burned from the activity. She slowed down, flipped over, and floated on her back, letting the water lap around her breasts. The feel of the water on her skin was sensual and soothing, but it was time to get out, towel off and get dressed before Sam returned. Mikaela turned and dove one last time, heading to the stairs.

Sam arrived home. He grabbed a cookie off the counter in the kitchen and headed to his bedroom to change. The dinner was still four hours away and the weather had become warm and sunny, so getting out of his suit became a priority. He shed his clothes and threw on shorts and a T-shirt. Mikaela wasn't inside, but he knew she had to be around because the Jeep was still in the garage. After grabbing another cookie from the kitchen, he wandered outside to find her.

He expected to find her reading on one of the deck chairs and was surprised to see them empty. He looked out at the lake, but it was quiet. The doors to the pool house were open, and when he paused to listen, he heard a rhythmic splashing. Sam wandered closer and stopped as Mikaela flipped onto her back and floated across the pool.

The gentlemanly thing would be to walk away and give her some privacy, he thought. She looked completely relaxed and stunningly beautiful. It was hard not to imagine how soft that skin would feel under him. How it would feel to run his hands down the smooth, slippery length of her body. How would she react if he joined her? Just slid in there with her? He watched her head for the stairs. Guiltily, he took a step back.

Her head whipped around with his movement and she slid back down into the water. "Hi. You're back early."

Sam shoved his hands in his pockets, grateful she couldn't read his mind. "Yeah, it didn't take as long as I thought it would. I guess everyone wanted to get out and enjoy the . . . weather," he said, trying to focus.

"Right, well . . . I decided to go for a swim."

"It looks inviting. I was thinking of joining you."

"I'm just getting out," she replied quickly.

"Oh . . . too bad."

She looked away, avoiding his eyes, and cleared her throat. "Well, if you could just turn around. I, ah, didn't have a swimsuit, and I'd like to grab a towel."

"I can get one for you."

"Yeah, thanks. But I think I'm good. If you could . . ." she said and twirled her finger, indicating he should turn around.

"You know, I am a doctor. I've seen naked women before."

"I'm sure you have. Being an *eye* surgeon and all," she drawled. "If you could just turn around?"

Sam grinned and spun around.

He didn't mean to watch. He hadn't intended to, but the combination of light and glass turned the windows into a mirror. The reflection was crystal clear as she took a deep breath, fanned herself, and walked up the stairs and over to the table with towels.

When she slipped, Sam started.

Mikaela caught herself and swore silently. He was watching? she thought with chagrin. She leaned over, picked up a towel, and drew the towel slowly up her body caressing her breasts as she went. "Okay, all ready," she purred.

Sam slowly turned and sauntered toward her. "Are you?"

"Hmmm . . . ?"

"Ready?"

"Well. I'm not completely dry. But I'm covered. It's a beautiful pool. I really enjoyed that."

Sam came and stood close enough to brush her arm holding the towel. "I'm glad you enjoyed it. I enjoyed it . . . I enjoy it, too."

Mikaela tried not to blush. She tilted her head and looked at him, considering. It would be good, no doubt about that. He looked good, standing there in casual shorts and T-shirt. He smelled good, and she wondered what he would taste like.

Dr. Eye Candy. Dr. Eye Candy, she repeated to herself. She was playing with fire and told herself to stop. But it was like a moth attracted to a flame. It was hard to back away from the heat.

"You look . . . hot," she whispered. "Maybe I can do something about that."

"What did you have in mind?" he asked, as interest flared in his eyes. He leaned closer until his chest brushed the towel covering her.

"This," Mikaela said, and with a firm push, sent him teetering backward into the pool. With a fast grin, he made a hasty grab for her, but she scooted out of reach. He lost his balance and landed with a splash.

Sam came up laughing and with a sweep of his arm across the surface, sent a spray of water her way.

Mikaela laughed and dashed out of its way to grab her clothes. "Just trying to help," she said innocently.

With two powerful strokes he swam to the shallow end and stood up. He pulled his soaking wet T-shirt over his head.

That stopped her. He was gorgeous in a suit and gorgeous in casual shorts and T-shirt, but the sight before her without a shirt had her humming. Broad shoulders to muscular arms, flat stomach to narrow hips was mmm . . . perfect. Mikaela almost dropped her towel, the need to feel his skin against hers so great.

Until she looked at his face. He was enjoying her reaction, expected it even, no doubt. With one fluid movement, Sam pulled himself up out of the pool and stood, with water dripping down his tanned chest.

Mikaela scrambled back. Hugging her clothes against her like a shield, she made a beeline for the doors.

"I'll need that towel back," he said.

Mikaela laughed and didn't stop. "I'll get right on that," she said, and waved as she headed toward the main house.

Sam watched her for a few steps then called after her. "Hey, Mikaela. Do you play tennis?"

She turned. "Yeah, I do."

"We still have a couple of hours. Would you like a game?"

"Sure, that sounds great. Let me get dressed."

"Or not," he said.

She laughed. "What?"

"We could play strip tennis."

"Strip tennis?" she repeated, looking at him in disbelief.

"Sure. I could even take a handicap, if you're scared," he said, tongue-in-cheek.

Weekly tennis lessons as a kid, summer camps, daily practices throughout high school, provincially ranked junior, varsity champ, she thought. "Do I look scared?"

"Just saying." He grinned.

"Is this how you usually get women naked, O'Brien?"

"I'm not the player you seem to think I am," he said. "In fact, I've never had a woman here before. And playing strip tennis with my brother doesn't have any appeal." Sam looked at her hungrily. "But you know, I'm all for trying new things . . . "

Mikaela shivered at his look. "I'm game," she managed. "But I'm starting with clothes on, and I would suggest you put on extra," she warned, and with a smile over her shoulder, went inside.

She pulled out a lacy bra and matching thong. Not her usual tennis attire, but she really wanted to wipe that smug look off his face. She pulled on a faded pink T-shirt and snug white shorts, socks and sneakers. Pulling her hair back in a ponytail, she grabbed her sunglasses and headed out.

Sam was waiting by the tennis courts with an extra racket. He had changed into dry shorts and shirt. He looked sexy in a backward baseball cap and sunglasses hiding his eyes.

He held out the racket and two soft, terry cloth wristbands. "Your handicap."

"Sure you don't want to keep those for yourself?"

He grinned and shook his head.

"Don't say I didn't warn you." She laughed as she put them on. She took the racket and tested it for the grip and weight. The feel was different from her own, but it was light, tightly strung, and fit her hand well.

Mikaela won the toss and had first serve.

She stepped over to her end, and positioning herself at the centerline, she tossed the ball in the air, getting a feel for it. With the next toss, she swung her racket up behind her head in a quick snap and sent the ball screaming over the net, bouncing inside the line, and top spinning out of bounds before Sam could react.

Sam stood up from his crouch and took his sunglasses off to look at her.

Mikaela grinned. "Lose the shirt, buddy," she shouted.

Sam shook his head and pulled his shirt off. "Enjoy it while you can, hotshot. It's not gonna last," he teased.

Mikaela enjoyed the view. Rippling muscles and the sheen of sweat never looked so good. Focus, she thought, focus. She wanted more.

Four serves later and a game under her belt, Mikaela watched as Sam threw his shoes over to join the pile with his sunglasses and hat.

"You're a ringer," he accused.

"Don't say I didn't warn you," she flashed back. "I did offer you the sweat bands, but you so chivalrously declined." She laughed.

She sashayed by him as they switched ends, wondering how he would react if she ran her hand over the muscles of his chest. It was getting harder and harder to ignore his perfect form.

Sam took his place at the centerline and bounced the ball, ready to take over the serve. “You’ve done it now. I’m not holding back any longer.”

Mikaela laughed.

Sam tossed the ball in the air, and Mikaela lost her concentration for just a moment as his muscles rippled in the sunlight.

The ball bounced and ricocheted out of bounds.

Sam smiled broadly. Mikaela eyed the ball with chagrin, as her attention came back to the game. She set down her racket and thought about removing one of the sweatbands. But instead, she shimmied out of her shorts and turned around to chase the ball, showing off the beauty of the thong. She came back and made a show of picking up her racket.

Sam sent a wild serve off the court and out of bounds. Men were so predictable, she thought. A second fault followed, and Mikaela smiled serenely as she chased the ball, looking forward to winning the pants off Sam.

Sam was down to his briefs and on the verge of losing the game when Mikaela shouted over. “Should’ve worn socks, O’Brien.”

Sam just smiled and raked his gaze from her head to her toes.

The next volley was hot. Mikaela wanted those briefs off. Watching a nearly naked Sam was torture. The muscles of his thighs rippled as he strained for the ball. It was all she could do to focus on the game. But she had a goal. Get his clothes off. Get her clothes off. Get him inside her. At thirty-love, she decided she no longer cared about being a statistic. She strained and rallied and cut across the court. Finally, with one last slam as her hormones raged, she sent the ball cracking across the court with a spin off to the right, as Sam pushed to the left.

Mikaela whooped and jumped in the air. “She wins,” she shouted, as she danced and wiggled her way to the net.

Sam stood at the net with his hands on his hips, grinning at her and shaking his head.

"This is better than winning the provincials and varsity title combined," she said.

"What?" Sam asked. "Provincials? Varsity? You could've said something."

"I could have, but that would've spoiled all the fun. Those briefs have got to go."

"I think you're enjoying this a little too much," he said. "And I'm not sure you won that fairly."

"Now, now. Don't be a sore loser. Fair's fair. I did warn you," she reminded him. "Do you need a hand with that?" she teased. "Or maybe you think it would be fairer if I did this," she said as she toed off her sneakers and slowly pulled her shirt over her head.

Sam looked at the lacy bra covering full breasts. His eyes roamed down to the curve of her hips with the scrap of fabric and came back to meet her eyes. He swallowed. "Losing never looked so good."

Mikaela walked toward the net, her heart skipping at the intensity of his gaze. Sam stood still as Mikaela reached up and placed her hands on his chest. She felt hard muscles and the steady beat of his heart.

"I need to hit the shower," he said softly.

"Or we could just get sweatier," she said. She ran her hands slowly down his chest, loving the feel of muscles rippling as she roamed down to his waistband.

She felt his breath quicken as he grabbed her wrists. He crushed his lips to hers. The need inside Mikaela's head exploded as she pressed against him and jumped into his arms. He lifted her over the net and she wrapped her legs around him. She ran her hands through his hair and held him close, nipping at his lower lip and tasting the saltiness of his skin. Closer, closer, was all she could think. Her breasts strained against his chest. He tasted the skin of her neck and sent shivers down her back.

Mikaela held on tight when he carried her to the pool and waded in with her in his arms. Gentle hands stroked the length of her legs, drawing down the wisp of fabric she wore. The clasp of her bra was next, and she closed her eyes as Sam ravished her breasts with his lips and tongue.

"You are beautiful," he breathed.

Sensation built inside her. It started as a slow swirl and built to a tornado of need. "Inside," she panted, opening her eyes and reaching for him.

She pushed herself up, clinging to his shoulders, then lowered herself, taking him inside. Water splashed to their rhythm until they exploded over the edge. Mikaela clung tightly as the orgasm ripped through her. She buried her head in his shoulder as the tremors subsided, and every muscle in her body went lax.

Sam kissed the top of her head. Gathering Mikaela close, he floated on his back.

Mikaela was overwhelmed with his gentle touch as he continued to stroke and soothe. Oddly and inexplicably, she felt an urge to cry. The sex was great. The best ever. Sam was great. And yet tears gathered in her eyes. In a panic, she desperately tried to pull it together before Sam noticed.

"Hey, are you okay?" Sam asked, slightly alarmed. "You're crying." He stood up, drawing Mikaela up to face him. "Did I hurt you?"

"No, not at all," Mikaela said, wiping the tears from her eyes. "It's just the chlorine. See," she said, wiping again, "I'm fine."

Sam looked unsure.

She couldn't meet his eyes. "I should probably go get ready."

She made to move, but Sam held her arm. "Are you sure you're okay?"

"Yeah, I'm fine. Better than fine," she corrected. "That was great," she said in a rush and reached up to kiss him.

Sam deepened the kiss. He couldn't help it. It was better than great. It was fucking amazing. Until he saw the tears.

Reluctantly, he pulled away. He never hurt a woman. Ever. One look at her face, at the look of embarrassment and panic, and he let it be. He watched her get out of the pool and wrap a towel around herself. She went outside and then into the house without a backward glance.

Fuck. What the fuck had he done?

He slapped the water. They'd have to talk about it. Obviously, not now. Fuck. After dinner, then. He heaved a sigh. It'd be right up there with having a root canal, but he needed to know what the hell happened.

It mattered.

She mattered.

Sam stood still as the thought sunk in. She mattered.

She was the most beautiful woman he had ever seen. She was fun to be with and made him laugh. She was easy with him. She wasn't awed by what he did or who he was. That had been a problem in the past. And she kept her word. He figured the odds were better than fifty percent that she would back out of this weekend. But she hadn't.

A painter, though? He never saw himself hooked up with a painter. Did it matter what she did?

Would she ever understand how unpredictable his lifestyle was? His hours were long, he never knew exactly when his day would finish, and being on call had ruined plans more than once. It made relationships . . . complicated. That's why he avoided them. He knew he had a reputation that was much more embellished than his actual score. But it had the advantage of self-selecting the ones who liked to keep it fun and easy, which worked for him. It always worked for him. Maybe he should stick with what worked and forget the rest.

Sam dove underwater. He hoped it would be that easy.

Chapter 6

Written in the Stars by Esmeralda Garnet

ARIES(March 21-April 19) Look at your situation from a different angle. Keep an open mind and don't limit what you can do because someone tampers with your confidence. Enjoy each moment.

Mikaela stood under the stream of hot water and sighed. Deep down, she knew what had triggered the tears, and she tried to wash away the feeling of sadness.

He was sneaky, Mikaela thought. He was charming and fun and had this single-minded focus that made you feel like you were the one. The sex was a mind-blowing twelve. That, she didn't regret. But what she didn't need, and hadn't wanted, was to lose her heart to him. The deal was to walk away after this weekend. It was only going to be a one-time thing. A weekend of fun.

She would accept being one of many. It was a twelve. So yeah, she would learn to live with that. What worried her was losing her heart to a guy like that. She did not want to fall in love with him. Guys like him weren't in it for the long haul. If she gave her heart away, it would be for the long haul. Sam was definitely not long haul material.

Mikaela lathered shampoo in her hair and scrubbed furiously. How did this happen? She had no intention of sleeping with him. She sighed again as she stood under the water and let it rinse away the suds. She knew how it happened. He was sexy and cute and she wanted him to touch her.

Physically touch her, she thought with chagrin. She didn't want him to touch her heart. She didn't want to care. That was annoying.

Well that's a lesson learned, Mikaela thought as she turned off the water and grabbed a towel. Men who have a reputation of being playboys get that reputation because they're good at it. They're charming and fun and make you feel like you're the only one who matters. And probably in that moment, you are.

She dried her hair and rubbed a scented lotion over her skin. Until the next attractive woman comes along and you're no longer in the moment.

Mikaela shimmied into a turquoise knit dress, with a scooped neck in front and draping in the back, and let it fall to mid-thigh, enjoying the way it clung to her curves and showed off long, toned legs. So she had two choices. She could either leave with regrets, which was hard to do because really, the sex was fantastic. Or she could suck it up, live in the moment, enjoy Sam's company and the fantastic sex for the weekend, and then move on. Lower her expectations, ignore the ache in her heart, and move on.

Mikaela pulled her hair back leaving loose curls to frame her face, then added dangling earrings and a matching turquoise crystal necklace. A silver bracelet at her wrist and a delicate silver anklet made her feel feminine and sexy. She stepped into high heels, grabbed her clutch, and checked the time. Six forty-five.

Here's to living in the moment, she thought, then went to find Sam.

Chapter 7

happenstance horoscope

ARIES (March 21-April 19) You've got what it takes to make things happen. Choose your direction and follow through. Build greater support by doing what's expected.

Sam was in the kitchen, leaning against the counter with his cell phone in his hand, when Mikaela came to find him. He straightened when he saw her. "You look beautiful," he said. He searched her face.

Mikaela couldn't hold his gaze. "Thank you," she replied. "You look . . ." *hot, sexy, good enough to eat.* Her brain came up with a lot of adjectives, but none that seemed appropriate. "Very handsome," she said finally, thinking she sounded lame, but safe.

He smiled and her heart melted. She was toast. Stay in the moment, she chided herself.

"You know," Sam said, with a gleam in his eye, moving closer. "We could always ditch the dinner and stay in tonight instead."

"Tempting, very tempting," she replied, trying to keep it light. "It does have the ring of career suicide for you, though."

"Yes, unfortunately, it does. That it does," he agreed. "Maybe we could just eat quickly."

She chuckled. "Sounds like a better plan."

"I wanted to give you this," he said, and reached for a small box.

He lifted the lid to show the most exquisite diamond ring she had ever seen. A round cut pink diamond, as wide as a baby's bellybutton, sparkled in a nest of white diamonds. A row of diamonds glittered around the band. She looked up at him with wide eyes.

"We're supposed to be engaged," he explained hastily. "I thought you should wear a ring. But if you'd rather not . . . "

"No, of course I will," she agreed. For a moment it felt real, and she struggled to rein in the yearning.

He held her left hand gently and slipped the ring on her finger. Her heart swirled, she couldn't help it. Live in the moment. "Okay," she said, a little too brightly. "Any other details I should know about tonight?"

"I'll fill you in on the drive there," Sam said. They settled into his Jaguar.

"Tonight we're having dinner with members of the board of directors. Last I heard, all ten were coming with their spouses. I've met Bill Truent, the board chairman, and Shamir Adubha, the treasurer. The rest are community members, mostly lawyers and financial advisors, I think, whom I've not met. But if they're anything like Bill and Shamir, they'll be welcoming and friendly."

"Have you told anyone anything about me or us?" Mikaela asked.

"I've told them I'm engaged, but that's it." He smiled at her. "That seemed enough."

"So what is our story?"

"Dunno," he replied. "We met, banged, liked it, and decided to get hitched," he drawled.

"How romantic," she said dryly. "But I think we better go with something a little more . . . sophisticated, if you really want this job."

"Okay, create away."

"We can't be perfectly honest, but I think we should stick as close to the truth as possible."

"Okay, how about we met, made love, and decided we couldn't live without each other."

She wished. "Or," she drawled. "We could say we met when I painted your house. We met six months ago and got engaged two months ago. Does that work?"

"Sounds good. When's your birthday?"

"What?"

"When's your birthday? It seems like something I should know."

"Oh. April tenth. When's yours?"

"November eighth."

"I know you have a brother who's an architect. What's his name? And what about the rest of your family?"

"His name is Jonathan. I also have a younger sister – Olivia. My parents live in Cannebury, but they spend the winters in Arizona. My dad's retired. He is or was, I guess, a general surgeon and my mom's a librarian. How about you?"

"I'm an only child. My parents are retired, but they keep pretty busy. Well, my dad's retired. My mom considers it her full-time job setting up blind dates for me."

Sam laughed. "And how does that work for you?"

"Not surprisingly, not that well."

"The advantage of having siblings," Sam commented. "Olivia is married to Ron and they have a new baby, Arielle. The wedding and baby gifts were actually expressions of my thanks for distracting Mom and Dad."

Mikaela laughed. "Good deal. You're lucky."

He looked over at her. "I am." Sam pulled into the restaurant parking lot. "Would you like me to drop you off at the front door?"

"No, I'd rather go in with you."

Sam pulled into a spot and got out to open her door.

"I really hope you get this position, Sam. Is there anything else I can do to help?"

Sam looked into her worried eyes and smiled. "Have a little faith in me, darling. Just be yourself and you'll dazzle them. And thank you again for doing this."

"You're welcome. Good luck," Mikaela said and hooking her arm in his, leaned in to enjoy being in the moment.

Chapter 8

Zodiac Zach – Don't leave home without him.

ARIES (March 21-April 19) Jump into action and take control of a situation that has the potential to turn sour if you don't intervene. Your calm authority will cause others to take notice.

The maître'd greeted them at the door and led them through the restaurant. The historic building had an elegant rustic ambiance with hanging leaded glass lanterns, a wall of exposed brick, and fresh flowers at every table. Candles flickered and light danced off the shine of a wide-planked hardwood floor. In a more intimate room at the back, a group of men stood next to a curved bar of richly dark wood. Water trickled down a copper sculpture, the sound quiet and soothing and complementing the soft jazz music filling the room.

As they entered the dining area, a short, balding man with a round face and wide smile immediately excused himself from the group and hurried over to greet them.

"Sam, welcome," he said, shaking Sam's hand firmly.

"Bill, thank you." Sam turned to Mikaela. "Bill, I'd like to introduce my fiancée, Mikaela Finn. Mikaela, Bill Truent, Chairman of the Board."

"Pleased to meet you, Mr. Truent," Mikaela said, extending her hand in greeting.

"Call me Bill. And it's a pleasure to meet you. We're so pleased you could come this weekend. Let me introduce you to the others." He gestured over toward the bar. "Would you like something to drink?"

"Perrier and lime would be wonderful. Thank you," said Mikaela.

"I can get that, Bill. Would you like anything?" Sam offered, gesturing to Bill's half empty glass.

"Thanks, but I'm still working on this one." Bill drew Mikaela over to the group of men standing by the bar and introduced her. By the time Sam returned with their drinks, three other couples had arrived and the introductions began again. Mikaela enjoyed the camaraderie of the group. They obviously knew each other well and enjoyed each other's company.

"And here are Jeff and Jessie," Bill said as the youngest couple in the group joined them.

"Sorry we're late," Jessie said. "It's my fault." She rubbed her bulging abdomen. "I like to think I have control, but Junior here has his own agenda."

"You're not late at all," Bill said, to reassure her. "We're just getting drinks."

Lively conversation started up again as introductions were repeated.

When the waiter indicated they should take their seats, Mikaela sat across from Sam. Throughout the four-course meal, she admired the way Sam charmed and engaged those around him. Occasionally he would catch her eye and smile at her, desire flashing in his eyes. That sent her pulse racing and the temperature in the room soaring. She struggled to remember they were in the middle of a crowded dining room.

It was easier to focus on the people sitting beside her. To her right was an elderly lady, who had been introduced as a board member.

"The board is really impressed with Sam," the woman said to Mikaela as dinner finished and people milled about the room.

Mikaela smiled. "He really wants this. It will be a loss for Rivermede, but a real gain for Emerson."

"Yes," the woman nodded. "Not everyone would be content to give that up or move to a small town."

"It's true," Mikaela acknowledged. "It's not a problem for Sam. He loves this town."

"How about you? Do you think you could settle in a small town?"

Mikaela tried to hide her surprise. "Yes," she said finally, realizing it was true. "I like the quiet and peace of it. I've only met a handful of people, but they all seem welcoming and friendly. There seems to be a close-knit community here."

"There is," the woman agreed. "People look out for each other. There's a sense of family," she paused, "which can be good or bad, depending on how close you want to be to your family." They shared a laugh.

Mikaela debated whether to ask the woman something that had been bothering her. How could she phrase it? "Is it a big decision to give out hospital privileges?"

"It depends," the woman said. "Some specialties end up generating revenue for the hospital, so it's an easy decision. But some, like ophthalmology, don't. In fact, because the turnover of patients is quick, when you balance the staff and equipment costs, it can end up costing the hospital money. We've been particular about balancing our books and keeping the hospital from running a deficit, and we'd like to keep it that way."

"Isn't the advantage of having eye surgery done locally a huge consideration?" Mikaela asked.

The woman sighed. "For some, for sure. Especially in the winter. But patients are rarely admitted for eye surgery. They're in and out the same day. So if you weigh convenience against the cost to the hospital, it doesn't tip the scale. I wish it did," she said, "but it just doesn't."

"That's disappointing," Mikaela said, her heart sinking for Sam.

The woman straightened. “That’s not to say we’re not considering it,” she said hastily, “but there’s more to it than meets the eye, so to speak.” She finished with a smile.

Mikaela nodded slowly.

Jeff, the young husband, rushed into the room. “Can anyone help deliver a baby?” he shouted. Heads turned, but he didn’t wait for an answer as he rushed out again.

Everyone started talking at once. Mikaela rose and looked for Sam. He was deep in conversation at the bar with other members of the board, so she grabbed her clutch and slipped out.

She spoke to the maître’d. “Someone asked for help?”

The maître’d mumbled something into a headset and quickly led her to an office across the foyer. Jessie sat on the floor supported by her husband. Her face was contorted with pain, and beads of sweat gathered on her forehead. Two of the restaurant staff hovered nearby.

They all looked at Mikaela when she entered. “I’m Dr. Finn. I’m an obstetrician.”

Relief flashed across the husband’s face. “Thank god.”

Mikaela smiled encouragingly. “The baby decided to come early?”

“I think so,” Jessie said, more comfortable now that the contraction had passed. “I’ve been having this vague back pain all day. Nothing major, more of a niggling pain. We considered canceling tonight, but then it stopped. But about fifteen minutes ago, my water broke, and the contractions started.”

“How far apart are they now?” Mikaela opened her clutch and took out a Red Cross CPR keychain she always carried with her. Inside was a pair of gloves.

“Two minutes. But I really feel like I have to push.”

Mikaela nodded. “I’d like to examine you.” She looked at the staff hovering nearby. “Could you get a blanket or a tablecloth? Maybe towels and some string?” She turned back to Jeff. “Have you called an ambulance?”

"I did, but they said we have to go to Rivermede. They said there's no doctor available here," Jeff said anxiously.

Mikaela put her hand on Jessie's belly. "Another contraction, Jessie. Just breathe through it. Don't push yet."

As the contraction eased, the staff returned with a blanket, tablecloth, and towels and handed them to Mikaela with shaking hands.

"Great. Now could you just stand at the door? I'm going to examine Jessie and I don't want anyone walking in. Unless it's the paramedics . . .

"How far along are you, Jessie?" Mikaela asked as she spread the tablecloth under Jessie and covered her with a blanket.

"Thirty-eight weeks."

"Any problems with the pregnancy?"

"No, none."

"And there's only one baby in there, right?" Mikaela smiled.

"Yes, just one," Jessie said, relaxing.

"Is this your first baby?"

"No. Second. We have a two-year-old at home."

"Okay. I'm going to feel inside, Jessie," she said as she slipped her fingers inside. "Was the first delivery this exciting?" Mikaela asked as she noted that Jessie was fully dilated and crowning.

"No," Jessie managed as the next contraction stopped her breath.

Sam burst into the room. "What's going on? What are you doing?"

"I'm delivering a baby," Mikaela said, distracted. She felt Jessie's abdomen and stretched the perineum as the contraction faded.

"You can't do that," Sam said.

"Yes, she can, you moron," Jessie screamed. Mikaela started. Sam stepped back. "She's an obstetrician. Who let you in?" she growled.

The waiter who had been guarding the door slithered up. “Sorry, so sorry,” he mumbled to Jessie. “He said he was a doctor,” he explained, and pushed Sam toward the door.

“Wait,” Sam said.

“Listen, man.” He mimed buttoning his lip. “Don’t wake the dragon,” he whispered to Sam, shifting worried eyes to Jessie.

“Mikaela,” Sam started and then stood frowning as he watched.

“Okay Jessie, one more push and we should get this baby delivered,” Mikaela said.

Jessie groaned with the next contraction.

A little head with a full mop of hair pushed through.

Mikaela gently wiped her hand over the nose and mouth, clearing the secretions away. She ran her finger down the back of the baby’s head and down the neck. And felt the cord wrapped around the neck. Her heart rate went up just a notch.

“Jessie, I don’t want you to push again just yet. Breathe and pant if you get another contraction.” Mikaela slipped her finger around the cord and stretched it over the baby’s head as she rotated the baby’s shoulders ninety degrees. The cord slipped around the shoulders and with a snap disappeared into the birth canal. “Okay, Jessie, one last push when you’re ready.”

Before the sentence was finished, Jessie pushed, and the baby slipped out into Mikaela’s waiting hands. She massaged the baby’s chest and the baby let out a wail.

“Beautiful,” Mikaela said. She watched the baby turn a healthy pink, and then placed her onto Jessie’s abdomen.

“A baby girl,” Mikaela said as she tied string on the cord in two places and turned to Jeff. “Do you want to cut the cord?” she asked, holding out scissors to him.

Jeff straightened with a tremulous smile and reached over to take the scissors. Mikaela held the cord between the ties as Jeff did the honors. Mikaela wrapped the newborn in a towel and handed the bundle back to Jessie.

Jessie took her daughter and hugged her close. “Oh she’s beautiful. She’s so perfect. Thank you,” she breathed. “Thank you.”

Mikaela took the scissors from Jeff’s limp hands and watched as he hugged Jessie and kissed her forehead. “She’s absolutely beautiful. Just like her mother.” He watched with wide eyes as the baby wrapped tiny fingers around the finger he held out.

“She’s so tiny,” Jessie said reverently.

Mikaela laid a hand on Jessie’s abdomen. “Almost done, Jessie. You’ll have another couple of contractions to deliver the placenta,” she explained.

Jessie nodded as she felt the pressure build again. “It’s not as bad,” she said, panting.

“No, but you might feel like pushing and that’s okay.”

Mikaela was examining the placenta as the paramedics arrived. She looked up toward the door as they came in, and noticed Sam by the door, watching her with a thoughtful expression. She probably had a bit of explaining to do, but more importantly, she needed to get Jessie to the hospital.

“I’m Dr. Finn,” she said to the paramedics. “As you can see, the baby’s been delivered and has good Apgar scores.”

“Maybe we could just skip the hospital altogether,” Jessie interrupted hopefully. Jeff frowned as he looked from his wife to Mikaela.

Mikaela looked at her. “The baby should be examined, and you have a small tear that should be repaired.”

Jessie nodded and Jeff visibly relaxed.

“Jessie, I think there’s a piece of the placenta still in the uterus.”

“Really?” Jessie said, looking resigned. “That happened with our son, too. I had to have a procedure to have it removed.”

Mikaela nodded. “It may still deliver spontaneously, but it’s a large enough piece that we may have to take you to the operating room.”

"Would you be able to do that?" Jessie asked, as Jeff squeezed her hand.

Mikaela hesitated and glanced at Sam. "Of course," she said. "I can come in the ambulance with you and admit you to St. Peter's. I'll make the arrangements while the paramedics get you ready."

She nodded to the paramedics who were checking Jessie's vitals and preparing her for the trip. Mikaela removed her gloves and tossed them in the mess.

She approached Sam and motioned for him to follow her into the foyer. He pushed himself away from the wall and followed her out the door.

She stopped in a quiet corner and turned around. "So," she said, trying to decide where to start.

"So," he repeated. "You're a doctor."

"Yes, an obstetrician-gynecologist." She tried to read his reaction.

"Yeah, I got that. Nice work in there, by the way."

"Thanks," Mikaela said, looking away, then back at Sam. "Sorry I didn't tell you."

"Why didn't you?"

She shrugged. "I don't know. It didn't come up and didn't seem important."

"You didn't think that someone might recognize you?"

Mikaela stiffened. "I never thought of that," she admitted. "I guess it's a moot point now," she said with a grimace.

"Yeah," Sam said, putting his hands in his pockets. "I'm sure everyone will have heard of you by tomorrow."

"Sam, I'm really sorry about this. I should go with her in the ambulance. I think she's going to need a D and C tonight."

Sam waved it aside. "Don't apologize. I get it," he said, frowning.

He gets it, but he doesn't like it, Mikaela thought. "It'll probably be late before I can take her to the OR, but I could drive back tomorrow for the brunch."

"Don't worry about it. The main players met you tonight and I think everyone will understand if you're not there tomorrow. It's not worth the trouble to drive back."

Mikaela looked at him, disappointment flooding her. "Okay, if you're sure." Sometimes medicine just sucked. "You'll bring my stuff back with you?"

"Yeah, will do. I'll get it to you," he promised.

Well, that was something at least, Mikaela thought. Mikaela looked over as the doors opened and the paramedics wheeled out a stretcher with Jessie and the baby.

"I should go."

"Sure," Sam said. "I hope it all goes smoothly."

"Thanks. Thanks for everything." She reached up and quickly kissed Sam's cheek, then spun on her heel and hurried after the paramedics.

Do not cry. Do not cry, she told herself sternly. Disappointment and regret washed over her. She looked up as the hotel staff held out her purse. She gave a tight smile and straightened her shoulders. Time to put on her Dr. Finn façade, she thought as she climbed into the back of the ambulance.

Chapter 9

Written in the Stars by Esmeralda Garnet

ARIES (March 21-April 19) Emotions will escalate and confusion will set in with regard to a partnership you thought you could count on. Take time to absorb what's happened. You are sitting in a much better position than you realize. Bide your time.

At two o'clock in the morning, Mikaela tiredly paid the taxi driver and let herself into her house.

Everything had gone well. The baby was examined and was fine. Jessie needed the extra procedure, but it went smoothly and the small tear was repaired. Both mom and baby were staying overnight in hospital and would be discharged in the morning.

Jessie was extremely grateful, embarrassingly so. Mikaela had tuned it out after a while, and the anesthetist had hardly paid attention. Unfortunately, the OR nurse had listened with an avid interest and egged Jessie on when Sam O'Brien's name was mentioned. Mikaela wondered if she should be worried about that. Probably should. Maybe tomorrow she would. Tonight, she was too tired to care.

Tired and disappointed and feeling like an idiot. So Sam could add another notch to his bedpost, the nurses would have food for their rumor mill, and she could work at mending her heart. Mikaela sighed. She had enjoyed being in the moment with Sam. In the moment, in his bed. On the tennis court, in the pool. The moments were all good, she thought sleepily. She just wished the moment lasted a bit longer.

One week later, Mikaela sat in Dr. Scott's waiting room, eyeing his secretary and tapping her foot impatiently.

What the hell was this all about? The secretary for the head of the Department of Obstetrics and Gynecology had called Mikaela's secretary and made arrangements for a meeting. Which was odd. They held monthly departmental meetings to weigh in on major issues. For minor matters, Scott usually caught them in the hallway between patients or dropped by at the end of a clinic.

So what was the deal with arranging a meeting? A formal meeting. In his office. It must be a big freakin' deal, but she had no idea what it was about. Mikaela felt like a resident again, being called into the head's office for an evaluation. Which was part of the problem of staying here long term. She didn't feel like a colleague, she felt like an underling. Again. She sighed in frustration.

The hospital clinic was a great set-up and Mikaela really liked the nurses and the support staff. They were all great – reliable and smart and fun to work with. She liked the clinics and the fact that someone else managed the staff, the supplies and all the administrative stuff. She had all the operating time she needed and the shared call worked well, so she didn't have to be on call twenty-four hours a day, seven days a week. It really was a golden job, especially for someone who feared change.

But the fact that she couldn't shake the aura of an underling was immensely frustrating. Mikaela couldn't imagine Scott summoning Dr. Engel or Dr. Parent like this. They had been in practice longer than she had been alive. She couldn't imagine either of them cooling their heels in his waiting room. She checked her watch again and thought about the patients who would be kept waiting when her afternoon clinic started late.

And who arranged a meeting without an agenda? What's with that? Wasn't it common courtesy to let the parties involved know what was going to be discussed so they could be prepared? Which she wasn't – probably. That was the problem. She wasn't prepared because she didn't know what this was all about, she thought with rising frustration.

Okay, deep breaths. Calm down. Starting off a meeting antagonistic and angry with the head was probably not the way to go. Look at the other side of the coin. Others seemed genuinely pleased to have her on board with the department. And she wouldn't have been asked to stay if they didn't respect her work. One would think. Mikaela sighed again.

"I'm very sorry about the wait, Dr. Finn," the secretary said, interrupting her thoughts. "You probably have a clinic to go to. Dr. Scott thought this conference call would only be twenty minutes. They must be running behind. Would it be more convenient for you to reschedule?"

Mikaela looked at the secretary. See, the respect was there. She just needed to wrap her head around it. "No, I'll wait a little longer," Mikaela said, too curious to postpone. "The clinic is scheduled to start at one thirty and the nurses will take a few minutes to get the patients ready. But thank you for offering."

"It's not a problem. If it gets too late, let me know." She smiled.

"Thanks," Mikaela said. As she checked her watch again, the door to the office swung open and Dr. Scott bustled through with an apologetic air.

Mikaela glanced up and, despite her nerves, smiled. Dr. Scott always reminded her of a snowman. His round face and balding head were a perfect match for his round middle.

Twinkling eyes, a button nose and a perpetual smile made her wonder if he kept a magical top hat.

"I'm very sorry to keep you waiting." He ushered her into his office. "That was a conference call and we were late starting due to 'technical difficulties,'" he said putting the last two words in air quotations. "Personally I suspect the crew out east just plain forgot, but it was important enough to wait until they sorted it out."

He gestured for Mikaela to sit down in one of the comfortable chairs in front of his large mahogany desk. "Please, sit down," he said and went behind his desk to seat himself. "Do you have a clinic booked this afternoon?"

"Yes, at one thirty."

"I won't hold you up too long," he said, slipping on wire-rimmed glasses and pulling a file folder over and opening it up. "First of all, I would like to extend my congratulations to you."

"Th—Thank you," Mikaela stammered. "For what?"

"On your engagement," he boomed heartily.

Mikaela's eyes widened and her smile faltered. "My engagement," she repeated.

"Yes, your engagement to Sam O'Brien," he announced. "O'Brien's a fine surgeon. You could do worse."

Mikaela blinked and stared. Was that appropriate? She thought not. But neither was lying to a hospital board of directors or the head, for that matter, so she wisely kept quiet. She frantically wondered how he knew and why he cared.

"Okay, well, thanks. If that's all," she said, starting to rise. The less said, the better. There was no need to tell him that she hadn't been in contact with Sam since she left in the ambulance with Jessie. Sam had dropped off her bag with her secretary and didn't that raise a few eyebrows. Mikaela had scooped it up and put it away, along with the speculation and curious looks. She did not want to go there with her staff. And Sam hadn't contacted her since. So fine. It was over. She was moving on.

"No, no, there's more," he said, skimming the letter in front of him.

Great, she thought as she sat down again.

"I also wanted to commend you for your dedication and hard work. You make us look good," he said with a wink. "I have a very complimentary letter here from Jessie Desarmes."

Uh-oh.

"She writes that you went beyond the call of duty when she went into labor in Emerson. She cites your professional and calm demeanor, your excellent skills in a less than ideal environment, your command of the situation, and your willingness to advocate for her when she needed to be admitted here, which meant the safe and healthy arrival of her daughter. She is very appreciative, very grateful," he said, peering at her over the rim of his glasses.

"I'm glad it all worked out so well."

"Yes, and in order to acknowledge how grateful she is, she has made a very generous donation to the hospital, and specifically to the Department of Obstetrics and Gynecology." He looked at Mikaela. "She states that you would not accept a gift and wanted to make this donation in your name."

"I'm honored. That's a lovely thing to do," Mikaela said, touched.

"It is. The board members here were thrilled and obviously want you to have input on how the money will be spent."

"Certainly, I would enjoy that," Mikaela agreed, worrying about where Jessie sent copies of the letter. Obviously to her department head and to St. Peter's Hospital Board of Directors. Hopefully that was it. She was going to have to contact Sam and 'break up' soon.

"Further, she wanted to let us know how excited she is that you'll be accompanying Dr. O'Brien when he moves to Emerson."

What?

He lowered his glasses. "Bill Truent is a golfing buddy of mine. He's been chairman of the board at Emerson for seven, eight years now. As a matter of fact, we were at a charity golfing event last weekend. He tells me that they were reluctant to take on an eye surgeon, but you were the icing on the cake for them. They've been trying to woo an ob-gyn there for years. They're absolutely delighted that you'll be headed their way."

"Oh, but . . ." Mikaela stammered, trying to think. "I didn't hear about a decision being made. And I don't think we ever discussed *me* going. It was really Sam's deal."

"It was news to me and I told him as much. But Fiona Harkness insisted that you mentioned you would be accompanying him."

"Fiona Harkness?"

"Yes, she's probably the most powerful board member there. She's a quiet soul, a diminutive woman. You'd never know it to talk to her, but she's got family money behind her. Family money that speaks."

Quiet soul, diminutive woman? The woman Mikaela sat beside during dinner? The one she pumped for information? Oh no. "Well, really sir, I don't want to make any hasty decisions or make any big changes—"

"Nonsense," Dr. Scott interrupted. "You'll have a great set up there. They're willing to modernize the equipment to your specifications. If I were twenty years younger I'd jump at this."

"Really, I think I . . ." she said as she tried to stop the tsunami of change.

"And because of your exemplary record, we'll continue to award you privileges here. It actually works out well. We have a new high-risk delivery fellow starting in November and he'll pick up your clinic and OR time. I was trying to juggle it all to make it work for him. Funny how it all works out, isn't it?"

Chapter 10

Zodiac Zach – Don't leave home without him.

ARIES (March 21-April 19) A proposal with potential to propel you forward should be considered. A sudden change will lead to a contract or alter the way you currently live. Love and romance are highlighted.

Dr. Scott had rambled on for another ten minutes, but Mikaela hadn't heard a word he'd said. She was still reeling from the shock. After he announced he was giving away her time, her mind went blank.

She was fired. Essentially. No operating room time. No clinic space. How had this happened? She would still have privileges, but big whoop. What good was that without being able to operate or have clinics?

This meant change. Big change. Big scary change. That she hadn't planned. Zodiac Zach and Esmeralda had warnings, but what about happenstance weighing in?

Mikaela stared blindly at her schedule for the afternoon clinic. How was she going to fix this?

Okay, she would go back and tell Dr. Scott that it was all a misunderstanding. Tell him she wasn't engaged to Sam. Tell him people just made that assumption when they showed up together. Haha, just kidding.

Mikaela groaned. They'd be caught in their lie. How would that look? Yeah, we lied so Sam could get the position he really wanted. Both hospitals and the medical licensing body would most certainly be unhappy with that behavior.

She could go back and tell Dr. Scott that she and Sam broke up. Tragic, but true, and now she needed her job back. That might jeopardize Sam's chances of moving to Emerson, but what about her job? She lost her job. That wasn't fair. And why should his job be more important than hers? They needed to fix this. *He* needed to fix this. He got her into this, and he needed to get her out.

Mikaela grabbed her cell phone and sent off a text to Sam.

We need to talk.

Done. Now she needed to take a deep breath, put it aside and focus on work. While she still had a job.

With barely concealed fury, Sam disconnected the call. That was not what he wanted to hear.

They were so delighted to welcome an obstetrician and gynecologist to Emerson. It was part of the hospital's long-term strategic plan to recruit one and they had incentives and bonus money. It was an underserviced specialty and they couldn't be happier to welcome Dr. Finn. Would she consider the position of head of obstetrics and gynecology, they wondered? Would she be able to help them update the delivery suite? They would guarantee her as much clinic and operating time as she needed.

And, oh yeah. He could come, too. They could probably find a half day every two weeks for him to operate. Probably. Maybe.

Sam was livid. He had been required to submit a ten page application, a resume, references, a background check, and verification of good standing from the College of Physicians and Surgeons. He had attended two formal interviews, presented rounds and had informal interviews at dinner and brunch that idiotic weekend, and this is what happened? What the fuck? That was it? Deliver one baby and that was it? Did anyone even check her credentials? She told him she was a painter, for God's sake.

Apparently, painters who deliver babies had more street cred than a fully qualified ophthalmologist with subspecialty training. Sam shook his head in disgust. Maybe he should rethink this whole thing. If that's what they considered a priority, maybe he should change his.

A little late for that. After that weekend, he was so sure of getting the job that he'd submitted his resignation and accepted an offer on his house. Everything had looked like a go. Several people had hinted that he was a shoe-in. He was told they were trying to draw specialists to the hospital. That they would never turn down an ophthalmologist. So what the hell happened? Who made those decisions? Certainly not the same people he talked to.

Huge disappointment sat on his shoulders. Sam really wanted change. He was so certain it was going to happen and now that the cottage was renovated, he wanted to be there. So he bit the bullet, and even though he thought it ridiculous, did the paperwork and jumped through the hoops.

For what?

To be told he was second choice to an obstetrician-gynecologist. Too bad there hadn't been an eye emergency that weekend. Fuck.

And why the hell didn't she mention she was a doctor? How could that not have come up? Granted they didn't talk much. His body stirred at the memory. Sam sighed in frustration. She didn't think it was important? She didn't think about the million things that could go wrong? He was doing just fine in his application until she came along and complicated everything. This was all her fault. If she had been straight with him, it never would have happened. So *she* could bloody well fix it.

He fired off a text.

We need to talk.

Before he had a chance to set his phone down, it beeped. He read Mikaela's text.

We need to talk.

He grunted. She probably heard about her sweet deal and wanted to gloat. He certainly wasn't going to be inconvenienced. He texted back.

Meet me at my office after work.

Her text came almost immediately. *No, not at the hospital.*

Fine, we can meet at Lango's at 7 p.m., he replied.

No, too public.

Sam shook his head. Really? More hoops? How could anyone so sexy, so smart, be so crazy?

Where would you like to meet?

Mikaela looked at the text, exasperated. She didn't want to meet. That was the problem. She wanted to pretend this whole thing didn't happen.

Where should they meet? Some place private to discuss their lies and deceit, she winced. She could invite him to her place. Hard to boot him out if she'd had enough, though. His place? She'd have control. That might work. If he still had a house in town.

Do you still have the place on Pinewood?

He replied, *Yes.*

Can we meet there?

Sure, I'll pick up some take-out.

It's not a date, O'Brien.

Agreed. I'll be eating pizza. If you want some, come at 7 p.m.

Fine, she texted and then put her cell phone down with a snap. She would not be charmed by those intense blue eyes or the thoughtful offer of pizza. She would not be swayed. She'd stand her ground and keep her privileges. It wasn't a date. It wasn't about the best sex she's ever had or her need to touch him again.

Mikaela shivered.

Yeah, she was sunk. She'd better start embracing change.

Chapter 11

happenstance horoscope

ARIES (March 21-April 19) Refuse to let an emotional incident stand between you and your success. A change of attitude and innovative methods will help you change your earning potential, allowing you greater freedom.

Mikaela pulled into Sam's driveway and parked the car. It was just a little after seven. It had been a long afternoon, and she had finished the clinic and all the paperwork that went along with it just twenty minutes ago.

She was tired and hungry . . . and tired. Driving over, she wondered why she thought they needed to talk. She could have sent a text to break up. Apparently couples did it all the time. As the afternoon wore on and her energy wore out she began to see the value. Break up and carry on. That should be her new mantra. They weren't even really together. So texting to break up made even more sense.

So why did the idea depress her? Maybe it wasn't the idea of breaking up that sat on her shoulders like a heavy weight. Although that did sting. Really, what made her sad was how her clinic and operating time could be given away so easily. No discussion, no warning, just boom. Gone. She thought she had been a valuable member of the department. She pulled her weight, had expertise, even went beyond the call of duty. On-call deliveries, emergency clinics, meetings, undergraduate teaching. She did it all. And did she ever complain? No. But the minute a new fellow needs clinic space and operating room time, she gets bumped. No discussion. The decision has been made. There's the door.

It was embarrassing and humiliating. That pretty much summed it up. She was embarrassed and humiliated and now she had to go and air it with Sam. So what was more embarrassing and humiliating than losing her hospital privileges? Discussing it with the person who dumped her after sleeping with her.

Great. Won't this be a fun evening? Mikaela thought as she dragged herself out of the car.

To make matters worse, even if she did tell Dr. Scott that she and Sam were no longer engaged, it might not make a difference. If he made promises to the new fellow, it might not matter one iota what her plans were. There might be no going back.

It just gets better and better, she thought drearily.

Mikaela thought about turning around and heading home. Except he promised pizza. She was hungry and it was the least he could do.

She knocked on the front door.

Sam pulled open the door. He'd heard the car pull up and wondered why it was taking her so long to come to the door. He thought she would be bouncing with energy and gloating about the offer she was given. The sarcastic comment died on his lips when he looked at her.

She looked pale and tired, with dark circles under her eyes. Her slumped shoulders and unhappy eyes were the exact opposite of what he expected.

Sam cocked his head to one side. "Tough day?"

Mikaela straightened her shoulders. "I've had better," she said. "But I've had worse."

Sam widened the door and gestured her inside. "I can take your jacket," he offered, as she stepped inside.

Mikaela looked around as Sam hung up her jacket. "Nice paint job."

"I've wondered about that. Is your partner a neurologist? Dermatologist?"

Mikaela laughed. "She could be. Margo is a businesswoman and an artist. We started the painting business in undergrad."

"Why were you here painting?" Sam asked, thinking about how it all started.

"Margo needed a hand. She doesn't ask for favors very often, well ever, really. But the woman who started the painting fell and hurt herself while Margo was out of town. They were under a deadline, so she called me to help out. I just came over and finished the bedroom." She shrugged.

Yeah, and now every time he looked at the new paint color in the bedroom, he thought of her. It was driving him crazy. He couldn't get her out of his mind. "You did a great job. It looks professional."

"Still got my skills," she quipped with a grin.

"For that and a few other things besides," Sam agreed, skimming his glance over her face and focusing on her lips.

Mikaela looked away and changed the subject. "We should talk about Emerson."

"Sure. Let's go to the kitchen. The pizza just arrived and I'm going to grab a beer. You want anything?" he asked casually at the risk of her wrath over making it a date.

She sighed. "Pizza sounds great."

"Want a beer?" he asked, "or a glass of wine?"

"I'd better not. Water or a soft drink would be great if you have it," she said as she followed him into the kitchen.

"Are you on call?"

"No, not tonight. I've actually signed out to another OB. I just don't want to drink and drive."

Or fall asleep at the wheel, Sam thought as he loaded two plates with pizza.

Mikaela looked around the kitchen curiously. Dark cherry mahogany cabinets gleamed in an efficient space interspersed with stainless steel appliances. Buttery yellow Silestone countertops brightened the kitchen, complemented the faint burgundy of the cabinets and made the traditional look of the cabinets feel modern. "Did your brother have a hand in the design of this kitchen, too?"

Sam looked around, surprised. "No, it's the work of the previous owners. I didn't change anything."

"It's beautiful. Traditional with a sunny feel," she said. She pulled out a bar stool and sat at the counter to watch.

"Help yourself to a soft drink from the mini-fridge there," he said and pointed to a drinks fridge tucked away at the end of the counter. "Or would you prefer water?" he asked as he set a plate in front of her.

"Water would be great." She inhaled appreciatively at the steaming pizza, fully loaded.

Sam poured her a drink and came around to sit beside her. "Enjoy," he said as he tucked in.

They ate in silence for the first few bites.

"So you must be pleased with the job offer from Emerson," Mikaela said, her tone faintly sarcastic.

Sam shrugged, thinking of the raw deal. "Be better if it didn't come with a price."

"What price?"

Sam ignored the question. "You must be pleased with the offer you received?" he suggested, trying to temper the bitterness.

"Pleased? I didn't want an offer. I wasn't looking for change. I didn't expect to be put in the middle of this mess."

"What? It's a great opportunity. It's a great community hospital. They want you to be the head of the department. They want to give you a free hand to redesign the obstetrical suite. And you get as much OR time as you want. What more could you possibly want?"

"To be the one who initiated the change. To have a choice."

"Seriously? You're given a golden opportunity and all you can do is moan that you didn't have to work for it? Yeah, poor you." He rolled his eyes.

Mikaela wiped her mouth, threw down the napkin, and sat straighter in her chair. "I was told today that as of November first, I no longer have clinic." She ticked each finger. "Or operating time at St. Peter's. I lost my job. And what about you? You get what you want, even if it means lying and cheating. So fine. You got what you wanted. You got your precious job in Emerson. But I am not going to continue in this web of lies and deceit—"

"Really?" He picked up his beer and waved it at her. "This from the woman who poses as a painter and ends up delivering a baby in the restaurant foyer. You're accusing me of lying?" Sam took a swig of beer and set the bottle down with a snap.

"I did not lie," she said with gritted teeth.

Sam took a deep breath and leaned back. "Look, like it or not, you're in this with me."

"Not."

"What?"

"Not. I like it NOT."

Sam shook his head. "Yeah, I get that. You're unhappy. But my offer from Emerson is contingent on you going, too."

"Not my problem. Tell them we broke up." She shrugged.

"Fine. Then we're both out of a job. Is that what you want?" He raised his hands in frustration.

Mikaela sat, fuming.

"Look. I'm not happy about how this turned out either," he said, more calmly. "But let's make the best of it."

Mikaela snorted.

"Let's accept the offer from Emerson," Sam suggested. "We'll give it a bit of time. I'll be able to get established and you can give this change a chance. If you hate it, I'll help you get your job back here."

"How much time?"

"I don't know," Sam said, rubbing a hand over tired eyes. "Three months, six months?"

"My time went to a new fellow who's supposed to be here for a year."

"Give it a year, then. Talk to your department head. Tell him that you'd like to take a year to decide if you like the smaller community. Ask him to give you first pass on the time when the fellow's year is up. Would he go for that?"

"Maybe," Mikaela admitted. "So much could happen in a year though."

"Have you considered that some change is good?"

Mikaela was silent. "I'll reserve judgment. What about our 'engagement'?"

"Might be easier to continue with that," Sam said thoughtfully. It didn't have anything to do with the fantastic sex or the need to see her, the fact that he enjoyed her company, he told himself. It just fit the plan. "Then if you do decide at some point that you don't like Emerson," he said, not really understanding how she couldn't like the sweet deal she'd been given, "we can 'break up' and you can use it as an excuse to come back. There's lots of room at my house."

Mikaela looked at him. "So we would live together at your place."

Sam nodded.

"You wouldn't mind us being together 24-7?"

Sam hardened at the thought and took a swig of beer. "No. Would it be a problem for you?"

"We spent a weekend together and after I left, you didn't call. I didn't hear from you until this," she waved her hand in the air, "fiasco unfolded. So I'm a little surprised that you're suggesting I move in with you."

Sam tried to downplay it, not wanting to scare her off, appreciating how much he needed her to agree. "Sure. It's a business arrangement." He shrugged. Didn't seem like a good time to mention that he hadn't been able to get her out of his head. That he hadn't wanted to go out with anyone since. That she was all he thought about. And that he wasn't entirely comfortable with any of it.

"A business arrangement," she repeated. "So all we share is space?"

"Sure."

Mikaela hid her disappointment. Obviously the mind-blowing sex they shared wasn't so mind blowing to him. She was just one of many. And apparently not the best. "Okay, then. I guess I'll see you on November first in Emerson." She finished her drink and stood up, trying to muster up some dignity. She made her way to the front door with Sam trailing.

"Mikaela?" Sam said as he held out her coat.

She turned to him as she shrugged into her coat.

"Thanks."

Mikaela just nodded and headed out. She drove home blindly, feeling numb.

She pulled into her driveway and unlocked the door from the garage. Throwing her coat on the hook, she turned off the light and climbed wearily upstairs to her bedroom. She peeled off her clothes, slipped into comforting flannel, brushed her teeth and fell into bed.

Her weary brain ached to settle. So to summarize, she thought tiredly, she'll be losing the security of her old job, moving to a new town, changing to a new hospital with new routines, new staff, and more call. She'll have more responsibility as department head, more meetings, greater challenges, and more decisions to make as she becomes responsible for creating a new delivery suite. And she'll be living with Sam. A shiver ran through her at the thought. He was so damn sexy. But it was a business arrangement. So she'll pretend to be in love with him to everyone else and pretend not to be in love with him, to him. For a year.

Sounded sufficiently complicated.

No wonder she feared change.

Chapter 12

Zodiac Zach – Don't leave home without him.

ARIES (March 21-April 19) Someone from your past will influence your future. Put greater emphasis on making personal changes that boost your confidence and make you feel good. Make time for pampering.

Mikaela settled back in the lounger and took a sip of the fruity ice drink decorated with a little umbrella and a mango-pineapple garnish. "Oh, that's delicious," she said, enjoying the sweet taste and the kick from the alcohol. She looked out at the turquoise water lapping up gently on the white sand, her whole body relaxed. "This is an island paradise," she said to Margo, who sat beside her slathering sunscreen on her arms and legs.

"I'm so glad we could get away," Margo commented. "I love it here. Here," she said to Mikaela, tossing her the sunscreen. "You should use this, too. It's lovely in the shade, but the sun is still pretty hot."

"I know," Mikaela said, grabbing the lotion. She set her drink down on a small table between them and smeared sunscreen on the exposed skin around her bikini. "Our last day – it would be a shame to get a sunburn now."

"We really have to go home tomorrow?" Margo asked as she adjusted her sunglasses.

"'Fraid so. And Monday I start at Emerson," Mikaela said with a sigh.

"How's all that going?" Margo asked, grateful for the opening. Mikaela hadn't wanted to talk about it all week and

Margo was getting worried about her. Mikaela had held her last clinic at St. Peter's on the Friday before they left, and she had been quiet and sad the first couple days of the holiday.

"It's going," Mikaela admitted. "Privileges for Emerson went through a few weeks ago. I've given them a template for booking the clinics. The first week will be light so I can meet the staff and get used to the setup. So that will be good. They've put together a committee for the upgrades of the obstetrical suite. I've met with them a couple of times already, and we've corresponded by email."

"How does that look? Is it a big job?" Margo asked.

"Actually, it looks great. They're really serious about going ahead with it. There are enough people involved to have some practical and unique input and not so many that a consensus is never reached. They've already got architects drawing up floor plans and an engineering firm hired. I think it will be a big job, but at least it feels like time spent on it is worthwhile. If I make suggestions, they incorporate the ideas."

Margo burrowed her feet in the sand, enjoying the feel of the hot surface and the cool relief of the deeper sand. "Sounds exciting. So how come you don't sound more excited?" she asked gently.

Mikaela winced. "I'm excited. Of course, I'm excited," she said. "Why wouldn't I be excited?" Mikaela added, shielding her eyes as she rested her head against the back of the chair.

"Good question. Why aren't you?" Margo picked up her drink from the table and slid the kiwi garnish off the skewer.

Mikaela was silent for a moment. "It's a big change. What if I don't like it? What if they don't like me? What if it turns out to be too much responsibility?" She glanced over at Margo with worry in her eyes.

Margo shrugged. "You delegate what you don't have time for or what you don't want to make time for. If you try it and don't like it, you move. And," she said with a smile, "it's pretty unlikely they won't like you. You're a likeable person."

Mikaela smiled back. "Thank you," she said batting her eyelashes. Then she sobered. "It's just such a lot to take in. I feel overwhelmed."

"Take one day at a time. Look forward to the challenge each day, and believe in yourself. You can do this, you know. You deliver babies for a living. Seems to me *that* comes with a lot more responsibility than organizing a department, meeting new people, and setting up a clinic."

She stirred her drink with the straw and continued. "You've always been a great team player, and you'll shine as a leader. And that's not something St. Peter's would have ever offered."

Mikaela stared at Margo. "Th—Thanks. It means a lot to me that you think that," she said slowly.

"Of course," Margo said, brushing it aside. "And when you hire someone to paint the new suite, I'll expect a call."

"Of course." Mikaela laughed.

"What did you decide to do with your condo?" Margo asked.

"I'm keeping it. Sam refused to take any money for rent or utilities."

"So basically you're going to be a kept woman." Margo raised her eyebrows and peered over the rim of her sunglasses.

"Yes, thank you for pointing that out. I am. But, the benefit is I can justify keeping my condo. Just in case . . . "

"Just in case?"

"Just in case I end up having meetings in the city or want to get away for a weekend. Or party with you." She grinned.

Margo grinned back and clinked the glass she was holding against Mikaela's. "I can drink to that," she said, taking a sip of the lime cooler. "Have you moved your stuff to Sam's yet?"

"No, I'll pack the car and move it on Sunday when I go."

"How has Sam been with all of this?" Margo asked.

"I don't really know," Mikaela said, looking out at the cloudless blue sky. "We haven't spoken since I told him I would go along with it. I assume he's happy about it. It's what he wanted."

"You haven't spoken to him since you agreed with it? Wasn't that like a month and a half ago?"

"Yup. Guess he's been busy. I know I've been."

"What?" Margo asked, feigning shock. "Here you're 'engaged,'" she said, making air quotations, "to Dr. Eye Candy and you haven't spoken to him in over a month. Girl, what are you thinking? I'd be acc-sex-ing those marital rights of mine, if I were you."

Mikaela laughed and shook her head. "I have no intention of acc-sex-ing anything. This is a business arrangement. We'll play it out for now, but when we break it off, and we will break it off eventually, I don't want to get hurt or have any regrets."

"But that's exactly my point. You should go for it, girl. Seize the day. You don't want to regret a missed opportunity. He could probably teach you a thing or two." Margo winked.

"He probably could," Mikaela agreed. "And that's the problem. He's a player and wouldn't ever settle for just me, and I'm not willing to share. It's better all round to avoid it altogether."

"Sure, you keep telling yourself that. But you know what they say about trying to have just one potato chip?"

"What?" Mikaela asked with a smirk.

"Once you've tasted their crunchy goodness, you have to have another, and before you know it the whole bag is gone."

"Good to know," Mikaela said, laughing and shaking her head. "I won't buy any potato chips."

"I think it's a little late for that. Have you told Sam about your parents yet?" Margo asked, eyeing the bodyguard who stood discreetly out of their view. It had taken a few trips to get used to the constant shadow, but now Margo was resigned to his presence whenever she traveled with Mikaela.

"No. Well, I've mentioned my dad's retired," Mikaela corrected.

"Your dad will never retire."

"Well, technically, he is retired. I just didn't mention from what, and Sam didn't ask."

"I'm surprised your dad didn't send out a team to check the security of Sam's place."

"He probably did. Or at least checked into Sam. But I haven't heard anything from him, and Sam's security is top-notch. As good, if not better, than my condo's."

"How much did you tell your parents?"

"I told them I was accepting a position at Emerson as the department head. They were thrilled for me."

"Naturally."

"And that I was moving in with Sam."

"Little trickier."

"Yes. They were pretty good about it. They did say they want to meet him at Christmas, though," Mikaela said, wincing.

"So you have two months."

"I figure by then, Sam will be secure in his new position, and we won't have to pretend we're engaged. I'll have a better idea about what I want to do, and who my father is won't be an issue."

"You're going to lie."

"No," Mikaela said heatedly. "I won't lie to Sam."

"You're just going to skirt around the issue."

"I like to think of it as the 'need to know' rule. If he needs to know, I'll tell him."

"But right now, he doesn't need to know," Margo surmised.

"Exactly."

Margo was silent.

Mikaela sighed. "What? I can sense your disapproval."

"Not really," Margo countered. "But don't you run the risk of getting into trouble by not being perfectly honest?"

Mikaela huffed. "You mean like exhibit A. The last time I used the 'need to know' rule, I ended up losing my job at St. Peter's, was coerced into accepting a position at Emerson where I'm going to have more responsibility, which potentially, and stressfully I might add, might be over my head. Plus I have a fake engagement with Sam, who, after having a mind-blowing weekend of sex, told me I could move in with him as a 'business arrangement.' You mean like that?"

"Ah, yeah," Margo agreed reluctantly.

"Yes, there is potential for trouble. But I don't care."

"Not every man is like Elliott," Margo said quietly.

"Maybe. Maybe not. It doesn't matter. One thing I can say about myself is that I learn from my mistakes. Elliott was a mistake, and I won't go through that again. Sam doesn't need to know about my father."

"I hear you. I just don't want you to get hurt," Margo said, squeezing Mikaela's hand. She hoped it wasn't too late.

"Thanks Margo. I promise to be careful.

"Come on," Mikaela said, grabbing Margo's hand and tugging her up. "A wise person told me to seize the day. Let's go cool off and enjoy the surf. No more worries about tomorrow."

"Woohoo," Margo yelled. "Race you to the water."

Chapter 13

Written in the Stars by Esmeralda Garnet
ARIES (March 21-April 19) Focus on the positive and be confident in new situations. Explore an opportunity that will allow you to grow. Embrace change.

Monday morning, Mikaela stood at the counter in Sam's kitchen eating a bowl of cereal. She scanned the newspaper and came to her horoscope. Embrace change.

Humph, she thought. No choice really.

Mikaela was dressed in navy slacks and a crisp white shirt. She tied her hair back in a sleek tail and put on a fine silver chain. She debated about the shoes. Business pumps or comfortable loafers? She expected some running around, so in the end chose low cut suede boots that were stylish and comfortable.

Well, Mikaela thought, she couldn't put it off any longer. She placed her bowl in the sink, grabbed her sweater and briefcase, and headed out to her car.

Sam had already left for the day. He was up and about an hour before her alarm went off. He had started at Emerson two weeks earlier and already had fully booked clinics.

She, on the other hand, had opted to take a much-needed vacation. In the first week, she packed up her office and finished outstanding paperwork. The second week was spent recharging with Margo in the sun. It was the best decision ever. She felt much steadier. She could hear Margo's voice telling her to think positively, take ownership of the day, and anticipate good things would happen. She could at least appear confident. Mikaela had been practicing positive self-talk all morning, some of it out loud, and was grateful Sam wasn't around to hear. Last night had been awkward enough.

Yesterday, she had decided what to bring and had squeezed it all into her car like a complicated tetras puzzle. She had cleaned her condo, emptied her fridge, and watered the plants. And headed out to Sam's place. She arrived in the early evening and Sam had been lounging in front of the television, watching a game and drinking a beer.

He helped her carry her stuff in and told her to take whatever space she needed, but it was awkward. They didn't really talk much and she escaped to her room to unpack. Later, when Mikaela went to the kitchen to put away some groceries, the game was finished, and Sam was heading to bed. Very awkward. They said good night awkwardly, and she went to bed thinking they were going to have to talk.

Later. She could only focus positive thoughts on so many things at once.

After an easy ten-minute drive, she pulled into the hospital parking lot. Free parking. One level paved parking lot. None of this circling around up eight floors to find a spot. How refreshing.

Mikaela parked her car and went through revolving doors to the reception area. She had a meeting with Shirley Carson from Human Resources at nine o'clock.

Mikaela walked over to the reception area where a middle-aged woman with a mop of curly red hair stood talking animatedly to a young woman behind the counter.

"Good morning. I have a meeting with Shirley Carson . . ." Mikaela began.

"Well, hello." The older woman turned her attention to Mikaela and held out her hand. "I'm Shirley Carson. You must be Dr. Finn," she beamed. "I'm very happy to meet you." She craned her neck to look up at Mikaela.

"My, you're a tall one, aren't you? Well, never mind. Welcome to Emerson Hospital." She pumped Mikaela's hand up and down. "We're so pleased you've decided to start a practice here. Oh my, you are going to be busy. I just found out my granddaughter is pregnant, now that's another story, let me tell you, but it's perfect timing because, you know, if she's going to get pregnant, it's a good thing she waited until we had a new obstetrician in town. How lucky is that? Isn't that perfect timing?"

Mikaela's head was spinning. "Yes, perfect."

"Well, let's not stand here chatting, we have a lot to do," she said as she led the way down the hallway.

"First, we'll get your identification organized, then I'll show you around. We've set up a lunch meeting with Doctors Grant, Kelt, and Marshall, the family doctors who do deliveries. And this afternoon you have a meeting with the chief of surgery. Can you think of anything else?" She looked up at Mikaela with a smiling face.

"No, that seems to cover it all," Mikaela replied.

They walked down a spacious, bright hallway with high ceilings and floor to ceiling windows looking out over green space and gardens.

"We have a lovely new garden," Shirley explained. "The hospital is forty years old, but we've done some extensive renovations in the last five years." She waved her hand toward the windows. "They opened this up and added the windows. Now it's bright and welcoming. It used to be quite dingy and dark," she added with a whisper.

They turned down a corridor to the left.

"Here are the administrative offices, the hospital CEO, Human Resources, and medical photography. We'll just pop in here to get your photo ID organized." She pushed open the door and greeted the young woman seated behind the desk. "Good morning, Trudy. How are you today?"

"Fine," said the woman. Her hair was pulled back severely in a bun and her young features contrasted with old, tired eyes. She didn't smile and barely made eye contact.

"This is Dr. Finn. She's starting today at the hospital."

"Fine," said Trudy in a low voice. "Stand at the blue line on the floor."

Shirley turned to Mikaela. "Would you like to fix your hair?"

"Ah, no. I think I'm good," Mikaela responded. What did her hair look like?

"Smile," said Trudy, with a deadpan expression.

Mikaela smiled.

"Sign this." Trudy pushed a contract across the counter.

Mikaela scanned the document and signed the bottom.

Trudy took it back without a word and ripped the bottom copy off. She walked back to the computer and with a few clicks printed off a photo. She flipped it over and adding a card with a hospital logo, slid the combination into a laminator. When it came out the other end, she punched a hole in the top and without wasting a single movement, slipped a clip through the top and handed it to Mikaela.

"Thank you," Mikaela said.

Trudy nodded. "It will be activated by five o'clock today. If there are any problems, bring it back."

"Thank you."

"Okay. All done here," Shirley said, holding the door open for Mikaela. "On to the next."

As they made their way down the hallway, Shirley glanced back at the office and whispered. "Trudy is also a public relations person for the hospital."

"Really?" asked Mikaela. "She seemed a little . . . reserved."

"You noticed that too, did you? I've always felt that way. But you know, with fundraising, she brought in over three-quarters of a million dollars for the hospital renovations," Shirley said with wide eyes.

"Wow, that's a lot of money."

"I know. I couldn't quite believe it myself when I heard that. But they say it's true. People must go for the quiet, serious type," she said shaking her head in wonder. "Now that's something I'll never be." She laughed. "Okay, next on the agenda. Your office. Have you seen it yet?"

"No, not yet. The whole wing was still under renovations when I was here a month ago."

"It's all up and running now. You're going to love it."

Shirley was right.

Her office was at the corner of the hospital on the same floor as the obstetrical wing. Light streamed in through a floor to ceiling window at one corner of the room, catching the polished wood of a large desk. Staggered floating shelves filled another wall above a long, low cabinet.

"Look at the detail on that cabinet," Mikaela exclaimed. "It's beautiful." She ran her hand along the inlaid wood that created an intricate pattern on the face of the cabinet.

Shirley beamed. "They did a great job. The furniture was all donated. People are really happy about having an upgrade to the obstetrical wing."

"Wow. That's very generous."

Shirley nodded. "Here are the keys for the lock."

They wandered down the hall and around the corner to the obstetrical suite. Shirley introduced Mikaela, rhyming off names and drawing everyone they met into the conversation.

Finally, Shirley glanced at the time. "We should head to the cafeteria to meet the community docs. Dr. Marshall's clinic starts at twelve thirty, so you'll have an hour to talk."

Mikaela waved to a chorus of good-byes. "I hope they won't expect me to remember all their names. I don't know how you do it."

"It makes a difference when you've been around as long as I have. I worked with some of their mothers and fathers," she said with a laugh. "But I'm sure it won't take you long.

"There they are," Shirley said and headed toward three people standing outside the cafeteria.

The two women were opposites. One tall and fair, with straight blonde hair that fell to her shoulders and the other petite, with short dark hair gelled into spikes. Both looked at her with cautious, curious eyes.

The male of the group had no such reservations. He smiled at Mikaela with a welcoming grin and threw out his hand for a handshake. "Hi, Ken Marshall," he said, pumping her hand. "You must be Mikaela Finn." He looked over at Shirley. "And how's my sweetheart?" He threw an arm around Shirley's shoulder and squeezed her close.

"Oh, get away with you." Shirley laughed and pushed him away.

"Will you join us for lunch?" he asked Shirley.

"Not today. But thank you for asking. I thought I'd let you get acquainted and iron out the details you'll need to get started. I know how hard it is to get you all together. Patty Kelt, Sylvie Grant. Mikaela Finn."

"Pleased to meet you," Mikaela said to each as she shook their hands.

"Lunch is the department's treat." She turned to Mikaela. "You're meeting with Bob Crispin at two o'clock and then that's it for the day. His office is on the fourth floor. Would you like me to come back and take you there?"

"Thank you, Shirley. But it isn't necessary. I'll find my way. Thank you so much for showing me around and introducing me to everyone today. It's been really helpful."

"Oh it's been my pleasure. If you need anything else you, don't be afraid to ask."

"I won't. Thank you."

Shirley followed them into the cafeteria and swiped them through the cash. With a cheerful wave, she bustled away.

Mikaela followed the others and they sat down at a table for four in a quiet corner.

"How long have you been at Emerson?" Mikaela asked.

Patty looked at Sylvie. "Two and half, three years?"

Sylvie nodded. "Yes, about that. It doesn't seem that long. And you were here a year or two before that, right Ken?"

Ken nodded. "I've been doing obstetrics for a year, but I've been here for about four years practicing family medicine. I had a lot of young women who wanted to start families and they didn't want to travel to Rivermede to deliver, so I ended up adding obstetrics to my practice."

"Do you share call?" Mikaela asked.

"We do. One night a week and one weekend in three. We tend to do our own deliveries, but it works out if we're away. Will you share call with us? Or just look after the high risk deliveries?"

"I'd like to share call and I can make a separate arrangement for any high risk deliveries." Mikaela took a bite of her salad.

"Great. That would work for us. We could each take one night and then the weekend call could include Friday. One weekend in four is better than one in three."

They spent the next hour discussing the details of their clinics and asking Mikaela's advice about their difficult patients.

Ken finished the last of his sandwich. "I've got to run. I've got a clinic booked this afternoon . . ." He trailed off when something caught the attention of Patty and Sylvie over his shoulder.

"That must be the new ophthalmologist," Patty whispered. "I heard he was gorgeous," she said with a sigh. "And they weren't exaggerating."

"Oh, wouldn't he be a tasty treat? Not many men make hospital greens look good," Sylvie agreed, flipping her hair and straightening her shoulders.

"I heard he was engaged. I wonder if that's her?"

"Tall, blonde and beautiful. Probably. They do make a

striking couple," Sylvie acknowledged, watching as the couple, both dressed in hospital greens, walked over to the cash.

Ken rolled his eyes as he stood, and Mikaela glanced over her shoulder to look.

Sam paid at the cash and then stood to one side, waiting for his companion. They did make a striking couple, Mikaela thought a bit peevishly, surprised at the stab of jealousy.

She gave a little wave and caught Sam's attention. Her heart skipped at the delight that lit his face. He spoke a few words to the woman. She continued on her way and Sam strode over to their table.

Mikaela stood up as he approached.

Sam threw Ken a curious look and then swung an arm around Mikaela's waist and leaned in. "Not sure if kissing in the cafeteria would be appropriate," he whispered in her ear.

"Likely not," she murmured. She turned and faced the group to make introductions. "Patty Kelt, Sylvie Grant, and Ken Marshall. My fiancée, Sam O'Brien," she introduced, slightly mollified to see the faint flush that spread to Sylvie's cheeks. Patty's eyes widened as she looked from Mikaela to Sam.

Ken smiled broadly and shook hands. "I've got to run," Ken said. "Nice meeting you, Sam."

"Same." Sam nodded.

"Would you like to join us, Sam?" Mikaela asked.

"Thanks, but I have to head back to the OR. I just came down to grab a bite to eat. How was your morning?"

"Good. Mostly orientation, housekeeping stuff. Patty, Sylvie, and Ken are the family doctors in town who do obstetrics so we were ironing out details."

"No easy task." Sam smiled. "I should head back. I'll see you at home tonight. Would you like to go out for dinner?"

"No, not really. I'd rather stay in. I shouldn't be too late."

He nodded. "Perfect, see you then." He gave her a quick kiss and winked, then headed out of the cafeteria.

Mikaela looked back at the admiration and speculation on Sylvie and Patty's faces.

"I have to apologize," Sylvie began.

"Me, too," Patty added. "We didn't realize . . . "

"No worries," Mikaela said, waving their apologies away. "I'll take it as a compliment. And I have to agree with you," she said with a grin. "He is a tasty dish."

Patty and Sylvie grinned and the ice was broken.

"Well, if you ever decide you want to share . . ." Sylvie hinted.

"Not gonna happen," Mikaela said without missing a beat.

Patty shook her head and drew Sylvie away. "Well, it was nice meeting you. We should get going too."

Mikaela nodded and watched them go.

Was that a taste of things to come? she wondered. Would she be spending her time chasing away hungry females and worrying about Sam's past?

Add it to the list of new responsibilities. Wasn't change fun?

Chapter 14

happenstance horoscope

ARIES (March 21-April 19) Proceed cautiously as you test the waters. Now is not the time to rush in headfirst. Take control, but avoid confrontation.

Mikaela pulled into the driveway at six that evening. Dusk had turned to darkness, but welcoming lights lit the walkway and front entrance. The afternoon had gone smoothly. She met Bob Crispin, the chief of surgery. He was a man of few words, but was respectful and diligent as he reviewed her paperwork and discussed department protocol. He confirmed she had two days a week to operate. That seemed to irk him, but that was the allotment to obstetrics and gynecology, and as the sole staff, she got it all. It was, in her mind, a double-edged sword. More operating time meant more patients. So she'd be busy.

And that, Mikaela decided, as she sat in the driveway, might be a good thing. More time at work meant less time at home, sharing a space with Sam. Last night when she arrived late and spent time putting things away in her room, she wasn't hiding in her bedroom, exactly. She just wanted to get settled before today. Perhaps it wasn't necessary to fold all of her underwear into triangles, make a symmetric pattern with her socks, or hang her clothing in alphabetical order. But it was justified, somehow. The option was to go out to the living room and relax with Sam as he watched the game on television.

Mikaela squared her shoulders. Today was a new day, and she would face him head on. Take control as happenstance suggested. She could handle this. Act perfectly natural. Set aside the fact that they had mind-blowing sex, and he hadn't called. Or texted. Or emailed. Set aside the fact that they had mind-blowing sex, and now he was sleeping down the hall from her. Set aside that he probably had mind-blowing sex with half the nurses at the hospital. Every time she met a female acquaintance of his, she wondered if they'd slept together. That irked her. Wasting energy being jealous irritated her even more.

And then she heard her mother's voice in her head. *If you don't like how you feel, change the way you think and act.*

Good advice, Mikaela sighed. But did that mean she should stop the jealous thoughts? Or should she seize the moment and ac-sex the fake fiancée rights, as Margo suggested? That probably wasn't what her mother had in mind.

Mikaela gathered up her briefcase and headed inside.

She was surprised to see Sam standing by the stovetop stirring a pot.

"Hi." He smiled. "You're home."

"Hi." Mikaela hesitated. "I'm later than I thought, but I stayed to organize my office."

"Did you get everything all settled?"

"Pretty much," she said. She set her briefcase aside and wandered over to the counter.

"I'm heating up spaghetti sauce, and the pasta will be ready in about five minutes if you want to change."

"You made dinner for me?"

Sam laughed. "Well, Mrs. Davy has the fridge well stocked, so I can't really claim to have made it. But I did heat it up," he said with a grin. "It can simmer longer if you don't want to eat right away. But if you've only had cafeteria food all day, I figured you might be hungry."

"I am. I'll go change." She started to walk to her bedroom and turned before she left the kitchen. "Sam? Thanks."

Sam gave a slow smile. "You're welcome."

Mikaela went to her room and replaced her suit with more comfortable yoga pants and a loose warm sweater. She pulled the band out of her hair and let it fall to her shoulders.

When she went back to the kitchen, Sam was draining the spaghetti in a cloud of steam. "I opened a bottle of wine if you'd like a glass," he said as he scooped the spaghetti onto two plates and added the sauce. He grated cheese on top and brought the steaming plates over to the table.

"That smells delicious," Mikaela said, her mouth watering.

"Mrs. Davy makes a mean bolognaise sauce," Sam agreed. He grabbed cutlery and napkins and, setting them on the table, gestured for her to sit down. "Bon appetite." He picked up his wine glass and clinked it with hers.

She sipped her wine and looked at him over the rim of her glass. "I wasn't sure if you'd be home yet. I thought you might still be at the hospital."

"I picked up OR time and finished at four. I did a bit of paperwork, but with no residents and no teaching," he grinned, "I was home by five. It's great. I had a swim, made dinner. And after dinner, I'm going to watch the game. I don't have to prepare rounds, work on research, or go to a meeting."

Mikaela looked at him. "You really love it here."

"I really do. I could use more OR time, but I love coming home to this," he said, waving his fork around the room. "How about you? How did it go for you today? Was it what you expected?"

Mikaela looked across at his beautiful blue eyes and gorgeous smile. She certainly hadn't expected to come home, share a meal, and sit and enjoy his company. "For the most part. I'm glad I met the docs doing obstetrics and sorted out call. I don't know if it's a small town thing, but the atmosphere was much more relaxed. And they all know each other, three generations back. I'm glad they'll be wearing name tags."

"Call everyone Junior. You'd probably be right."

"I know." She laughed. "They're all related. There seems to be a certain pride in what they do for patients. I like that. I expected to feel like an outsider or, I don't know, like I would have to prove myself somehow. But it's not like that at all. Generally, it seems, people are genuinely happy to have me here."

Sam nodded. "They are. I had a few people mention it to me, too. You'll be as busy as you want to be."

Mikaela nodded. "I'm taking call on Tuesday nights for the group so I was thinking of taking Wednesdays off, at least occasionally."

"Good idea. It's easier to add a clinic if you want more work, and it's hard to cut back once your schedule is set. I keep Monday afternoons open, and I've managed to snag some extra OR time. It's a bonus."

"So I can expect dinners made for me every Monday?" Mikaela laughed.

"As long as Mrs. Davy stocks the fridge, I'm your man."

Mikaela's heart swirled. "Well, we better keep Mrs. Davy happy then," she said lightly. "This is really good."

"Save room for chocolate chip cookies."

Mikaela groaned. "I can't resist, but I'm going to need to swim off the calories."

Sam looked at her. "Did you bring a swimsuit?"

Mikaela looked away and tried not to squirm at the memory of the last swim they shared. "Yes, I did," she said. "Is it okay if I use the study?" she asked, trying to steer the conversation to safer ground.

"Sure." Sam shrugged. "Just push any papers aside."

"Thanks. I'd like to look over some plans for the new wing tonight. They want to move ahead with the next phase." Mikaela picked up her plate and took it over to the sink to rinse it. "Maybe I'll take the rest of my wine in there," she said, suddenly anxious to leave. "Thanks again for dinner." She grabbed her briefcase and headed to the study.

Mikaela heard Sam rinse his plate and set it in the dishwasher, and then turn the television on to watch the game. Mikaela sat looking at the plans, not really seeing them. This was going to be harder than she thought. There were too many memories of the weekend here together and too much hurt along with it. She was going to have to harden her heart and pick up her self-esteem, or it was going to be a very long year.

Chapter 15

Written in the Stars by Esmeralda Garnet

ARIES (March 21-April 19) Take time to recharge. Put energy into something that makes you stronger mentally and physically. Don't jump to conclusions or take action in haste.

Mikaela yawned and rolled over, snuggling into the soft blankets and pulling the warm duvet up over her head. She had been at Emerson for a month and this was her first Wednesday off. She sighed contentedly. She had the whole day to indulge herself.

Mikaela had been busy with call the night before, and had fallen into bed at three in the morning. The last delivery, with twins, had been the most hectic. In the end they had popped out without a hitch and the neonatal teams, one for each twin, had been wonderful. It was the first delivery in one of the newly designed obstetrical suites. Doctor and nurse teams, and all the equipment for each of the babies, fit comfortably. It was efficient and managed to mimic a home delivery hidden in a very high tech, state-of-the-art world. She'd made a note to make a couple of minor adjustments, but overall, it was good. Really good. Over the next six weeks, three more rooms would be converted, and then things would settle down. But so far, the staff had been extremely patient with the upheaval, and the patients loved the changes. It was definitely worth the time and trouble.

But today, Mikaela wasn't going to think about work. She had signed her call over and left all the paperwork at the office. It could wait a day. She curled into the blankets and smiled at the thought of having the house to herself. Sam was at work. She wished she wasn't so attuned to his movements, so aware of him. But unfortunately, that wasn't getting any easier.

If they happened to see each other at the hospital, he would lightly hold her or kiss her quickly. He would speak quietly in her ear. To the outside world, he definitely acted like the besotted fiancé. Maybe his motive was to keep up the charade of their engagement, but he really didn't give anyone reason to doubt it.

They shared dinner together most nights. He would prepare something or she would, depending on who arrived home first. Mostly it meant warming up Mrs. Davy's meals. *Thank you, Mrs. Davy.* Mikaela hadn't met her yet, but every Tuesday the house was cleaned and the fridge and freezer stocked. Bless her heart.

She was secretly surprised Sam was home most evenings, but she loved it. She loved sharing her day with someone and loved hearing about his. She could talk to him about everything from hospital politics to patient care, and he got it. He didn't try to solve her problems. He asked questions and listened. It was refreshing and just made her happy that he cared.

Mikaela laughed and hugged herself. Sam O'Brien, well-respected eye surgeon, with the sparkling eyes and amazing smile, was interested in *her*. He made her dinner. Regularly. Who'd have thought?

When dinner was over, they would go their separate ways. Mikaela generally holed away in the study looking over architect drawings, planning meetings, or reading the latest medical journals. Sam usually went for a swim, and despite all she had to do, most of her time was spent trying not to picture him stripped down. Mikaela thought about joining him, but it was fleeting. When they were alone, he hadn't touched her. They had a sort of truce going, and despite its tenuous hold, she didn't want to rock the boat.

Once or twice Mikaela caught a hungry look in his eyes when he thought she wasn't looking, but he certainly didn't act on it. If the air sizzled when they were together, she tried to ignore it. Mikaela threw herself into work and Sam, it appeared, threw himself into exercise. The more she got to know him, the more time she spent with him, the deeper her feelings and the more she wanted him. It was driving her crazy, and eventually she would have to deal with it.

But today, Mikaela wasn't going to think about it. She would be content that they shared their space and their meals. Wondering what he felt for her and wondering what to do about her feelings could wait another day.

So how was she going to spend her day? Mikaela rolled over and stretched. First, she'd have a leisurely breakfast of French toast and strong coffee. Then, she'd try out some of Sam's very impressive exercise equipment. Free weights or machines? She laughed, hoping that was going to be the biggest decision of her day. She would definitely go for a swim and sit by the fire and read. She had a new Nora Roberts novel, something she could curl up with until it was time to eat again. Her mouth watered at the thought of Mrs. Davy's delicious lunch waiting in the refrigerator. Eat, exercise and relax, Mikaela thought. It sounded like the perfect day.

Mikaela pushed back the covers and glanced at the clock. Eleven o'clock already? She could probably skip the strong coffee.

Mikaela pulled open the curtains and looked with delight at the snow falling. Big fluffy flakes slowly swirled down and covered the ground with the first snowfall of the season. It was just the beginning of December, and the air was cool enough for the snow to stay. Perfect weather for a cozy day inside. Mikaela shrugged into a warm housecoat, pulled on thick socks, and headed to the kitchen.

As she licked the maple syrup off her fingers, Mikaela scanned the news and marveled how it was all about living in the moment. Today, it turns out, we should build a pipeline, depend on wind farm energy, and use wine to prevent heart disease. Last month, last year, it was all about the oil spill, windmills causing health problems and wine linked to liver failure. Really, life was one big gamble. You had to make the most of it and hope you were making the right decisions.

And that, Mikaela thought as she rinsed her dishes and loaded the dishwasher, pretty much summed up what she was doing. She hoped this would all work out. The job, what she had with Sam — whatever it was, she hoped she wouldn't regret it. Shaking off the mood, Mikaela went to get dressed.

An hour later, sweating, Mikaela thought the one thing she would not regret was living at Sam's place. His workout room was sweet. How spoiled could you be? Elliptical, rowing machine, free weights, so much to choose from. She ran, did lunges, bicep curls, and burpees all while watching the snow lazily and steadily covering the trees through a wall of windows. It was like a different world, miles away from reality.

A swim was next. Skinny-dipping crossed her mind, but was quickly squashed. Layers of stress melted away as she skimmed through the water. Relaxed and content, she floated on her back and watched the snow fall on the glass above. It melted as it landed and slid slowly down the sides of the pool house.

Mikaela waded up the stairs of the shallow end and wrapped herself in a warm, plush towel. Snow gathered on the ground, even as waves crashed on the shore. Sounds of summer and scenes of winter, nature made it work.

With all the exercise, she'd built up an appetite and enjoyed a roasted vegetable sandwich on thick ciabatta bread for lunch. She had just finished wiping the kitchen table, when she heard a noise at the front door. There was a brisk knock, and before she could make a move to answer, the locks disengaged.

Mikaela froze. She could hear her father's voice echoing in her head, and instinct kicked in. She grabbed a knife off the counter and ducked down. Heart pounding, she inched her way along the counter until she couldn't go any further.

"Yoo-hoo. Sam. Are you home?" a cheerful voice shouted into the quiet.

Mikaela's shoulders sagged in relief. Mrs. Davy? But now what?

Stand up and scare the poor woman? Or get up and act naturally? Like she regularly spent time squatting behind the counter branding a kitchen knife. She grimaced.

Mikaela stood up quickly and laid the knife on the counter just as the woman entered the kitchen.

The woman jumped and gave a little scream. "Oh," she said. "I beg your pardon. I didn't think anyone was home."

"Sorry," Mikaela replied, trying to reassure her. "Mrs. Davy? I'm Mikaela Finn," she said as she extended her hand to shake hello.

"Oh," said the woman, looking confused. "I'm pleased to meet you. But I'm not Mrs. Davy."

"Oh," said Mikaela, tensing again and itching to pick up the knife. "Who are you?"

Before the woman could answer, a tall man with gray hair at the temples, deep blue eyes, and a welcoming smile walked into the room. Mikaela took a step back. The man standing in front of her was the handsome spitting image of Sam, twenty years into the future.

"You must be Sam's parents," Mikaela said.

"We're Sam's parents," the woman said at the same time. "Sorry to barge in like this. We expected Sam to be at the clinic. I'm Marla and this is Walt."

"Hi," said Mikaela hesitantly. "I'm Mikaela." Her mind raced. What had Sam told them? Silently she cursed Sam for not warning her about their visit. "I'm pleased to meet you."

As Mikaela leaned over to shake Walt's hand, Marla gasped. "Oh my goodness! The ring." Marla exclaimed, her eyes wide. "Are you engaged to Sam?"

Shit, Mikaela thought. Yes. No. Yes. What would she like to hear? Yikes.

"That ring," Marla said, "was my mother's. She gave it to Sam. And he's given it to you," she ended tearfully.

Mikaela handed her a tissue. "I take it Sam didn't tell you."

"No, he didn't. But that's just like him. He wouldn't like the fuss," she said wiping her eyes. "But I'm delighted. We've been nudging Sam to settle down for ages now. We'd almost lost hope. And here he's been busy behind the scenes, and not mentioned a word. That would be so like him. That's why we make it a point to drop in and visit. I don't think we'd know what's going on with him otherwise. Oh, I know he's busy and all that, but really you'd think he could keep his mother up-to-date." She frowned and shook her head. "But never mind. It was worth the wait. Welcome to the family." She walked around the counter to give Mikaela a hug.

Walt followed Marla and gave Mikaela a hug as well. "It's a pleasure to meet you," he said with a smile.

Mikaela closed her eyes and wondered if this would be a good time to be honest.

"I want to hear all about you and the wedding plans," Marla insisted. "But just let us get settled first. Did Sam mention that we would be visiting?"

"No, he didn't," Mikaela admitted.

"Silly boy," Marla chastised. "Well, to give him credit, we actually intended to arrive this weekend, but with the weather closing in, we decided to come a bit early. We're on our way to Arizona. We take the Winnebago every year for the worst part of winter. Get away from all the shoveling and cold, you know. We usually get away earlier, but with Olivia, that's our daughter, having a baby we stayed. She had her about a month ago, but you probably know that. Cutest little pumpkin, she is. Arielle, they named her. So adorable. It's hard to leave, but we have a spot reserved in Arizona and we don't want to lose it. We always stop when we're passing through and stay a few days. I hope that's okay with you?"

"Oh, of course," Mikaela said quickly, trying to keep up. "You're more than welcome. You'll want the guest room. I've just stored a few things there, but if you give me a moment, I'll get it cleared out for you."

"Well, normally we'd say not to bother. We usually sleep in the Winnebago. But with the weather so cold, maybe we will take you up on the offer."

"Not a problem. It'll just take a minute to clear some space and put some fresh sheets on the bed. Do you need help carrying your things in?"

"Oh Walt has that covered. Thank you, dear. I'll freshen up in the powder room."

Shit, Mikaela thought. She gathered up the clothes in the closet, hangers and all, and dumped them on the bed in Sam's room. No time to figure out where to put everything now. She raced back and swept the makeup scattered on the bathroom counter into a bag. She pulled a suitcase from under the bed and emptied the dresser drawers into it. Zipping it up, she carried it to Sam's room and grabbed fresh sheets from the hall closet on her way back to the guest room.

She stripped the bed and made it again. She found new pillows in the closet and straightening the duvet, looked around the room. No trace of her. It was that easy. Focus on the positive, she chided herself. His parents needed a room. This way she could focus all her worrying on the new sleeping arrangements. And how much lying she would need to do to get through the visit.

Mikaela gathered up the dirty linens, carried them to Sam's room, and threw them in a hamper. She pulled out her cell phone and fired off a text to Sam.

Your parents are here.

After a moment, her phone lit up with Sam's reply.

What? My parents?

Yes. Your parents. What have you told them about us?

Shit. I'm sorry. I completely forgot they were coming. I actually haven't told them anything about us.

Nothing? Ouch. Before she could text back, he sent another.

I thought it would be too complicated.

Well it just got complicated. How long will they stay?

I don't know. Usually it's just a couple of days.

How much do you want them to know?

We don't have to tell them we're engaged.

Mikaela grimaced. *Too late. Your mom noticed the ring.*

Oh. Well let's just play along right now. We can discuss it when I get home.

Fine. Get here as soon as you can.

Just finishing the clinic. Shouldn't be more than an hour.

Mikaela's heart sank. So much for her relaxing day. It didn't look like she'd be reading that novel by the fire, any time soon. How much trouble could she get into in an hour? How many questions would she have to lie through? Maybe she could feign a delivery. Have an urgent call. Mikaela sat down on the bed and looked out the window. The snow was falling heavily and the roads would probably be slick. She wasn't going to go anywhere.

And really, *now* she worried about lying to someone about their engagement? Let's see, she's lied to her old department head, the board of directors at Emerson, the new chief of surgery, all the staff, her patients, her peers, and her parents. After all that, should she really be nervous about adding Sam's parents to the list? Mikaela wiped damp palms on her thighs. Yes, yes she should. She knew she risked being hurt by this deception. But at the end of the day, she didn't want to hurt anyone else. And Sam's mom had looked so touched about the ring. Mikaela twisted it nervously around her finger. It obviously meant a lot. Why would Sam give it to her? Why not some cheap make-believe ring to go with their make-believe story? Questions for another day, she sighed. Right now she needed to go and continue this charade and deceive Sam's parents. Convincingly.

But someday, she vowed, setting the cell phone on the dresser before heading back to the kitchen, things would have to change.

Chapter 16

Zodiac Zach – Don't leave home without him.

ARIES (March 21-April 19) Love is in the stars. Gather more information and be ready to counter opposition that arises. Now is not the time to be perfectly honest.

Marla looked comfortable in the kitchen, emptying a cooler of food into the refrigerator. "I brought some fried chicken and potato salad for dinner." Her gaze swept over Mikaela. "I hope you're not one of those skinny girls who's afraid to eat."

"No, not at all," Mikaela responded. She eyed the rapidly dwindling cookie jar. "I'm happy to eat anything someone else makes."

"That's good. I always try to bring something with me when we visit Sam. He's a great one for heading out to restaurants, but he appreciates a home-cooked meal. You probably already know that," she said with a smile. "I'll just finish putting these things away, and then you and I can sit and get to know each other. I put the kettle on for a cup of tea. Would you like one, too?"

"Sure, that'd be great. Thanks. I'll get the teapot out. Will Walt join us?" Mikaela stood for a moment trying to remember where it was stored.

"He's already out having a swim. He loves the pool, especially after that long drive. He worried you might think it rude, but I assured him we would have a nice little chat, and he could join us later. You don't mind, do you?"

"No, not at all." Mikaela set out cups and found the sugar and cream. When the kettle whistled, she poured the water into the teapot and added the teabags. Marla set cookies out on a plate and carried them over to the table in the nook.

As they stirred their tea, Marla leaned forward with excited eyes. "I want to know all the details. What's your sign?"

Mikaela blinked. "My sign?"

"Yes. You know, Sam is a Scorpio. I hope you're not a Virgo. All the Virgos are a little . . . zealous. Too much energy, if you ask me. And I don't know that Pisces would be a good fit either. They tend to daydream the day away, don't you think? I think Sam needs someone a little more grounded. Taurus would be okay, but they do tend to be a bit stubborn. And Leo, well, I think a Leo would be a bit too boisterous, maybe a bit too bossy for Sam. I wouldn't like to see another Scorpio. Can you imagine? That would be the worst kind of clash. Don't you think? Now, last year, I would have said Sagittarius. It was a good year for Sagittarius. This year, I'm thinking a Libra or Aquarius would be good. I could see that working. I've given this a lot of thought. I've told Sam. I told him he has to watch the sign, but I never know if he really listens."

Mikaela's head spun. "I'm an Aries."

"Oh perfect." Marla clapped her hands. "That's a good match, especially this year. The moon cycle is perfect for an Aries-Scorpio match. I've always thought Aries was best at thinking things through before they do something irreversible. That will be the perfect balance to Sam's Scorpio impulsiveness," she announced confidently.

Mikaela almost burst out laughing. Yup, that's her all right. Thinking things through. Planning change. Avoiding the irreversible. Marla's nailed it, she thought. Sam really should have paid more attention to the sign.

"What is your Chinese zodiac?"

"Pardon?"

"You know. Your heavenly stem, your earthly branch, your animal, your element?"

"I'm not really sure."

"Hmmm. We'll have to figure that out. Sam is a Tiger. At least he's born a Tiger. Personally, internally I think he's a dragon. Truly there is a bit of ox and secretively, I suspect a little goat. But then I'm his mother." She patted Mikaela's hand. "So if you were a horse, dog, or dragon, that would be wonderful. Oh dear, I do hope you're not a monkey. That would not be good."

"I'm pretty sure I'm not a monkey," Mikaela assured her.

"That's a relief. There are so many things to think about when you choose a mate. Are you a yin or yang?"

"Yin?" Mikaela guessed, hoping to make Marla happy.

"Perfect," Marla beamed. "Sam's a yang. The perfect match. You know Olivia and Ron are yang-yang so I do worry. But they produced the most beautiful daughter. Just goes to show there's something good there somewhere.

"And what is your favorite color?" Marla asked earnestly.

Seriously? She was engaged to her son and that's what she thought was important? She was beginning to understand why Walt went for a swim. "Ah, aquamarine?"

"Oh, aquamarine," Marla repeated, nodding her head. "Now would that be more blue or more green?"

Mikaela just stared. "Blue?" she guessed.

"Oh lovely. I love blue, too."

"That's important to finding someone compatible?" Mikaela asked skeptically.

Marla laughed. "No, now that would be silly, dear. No, I just asked because I enjoy quilting in my spare time, and I've decided to make a quilt for each of the kids as a wedding present. So yours shall be blue. And I'll get started on that right away." She munched on a cookie. "Have you picked a date for the wedding?"

"Ah, no, not really. We want to take our time and do it right," Mikaela said vaguely.

"Yes, that's the best way. That's the Aries in you. You're the planner. In the end, I'm sure it will be beautiful and exactly what you want."

Exactly what I want? Mikaela thought and sighed. "I hope so."

Marla was about to ask another question, but the sight of Walt coming into the kitchen interrupted her. He had changed into jeans and a warm sweater. Dark hair brushing his shoulders was still damp. "Now Marla, I hope you're not bombarding Mikaela with questions," he said, squeezing Marla's shoulder.

Marla reached up and covered his hand with her own. "Not at all," Marla replied. "We're just getting to know one another."

"I should apologize for heading out for a swim, but the pool is irresistible. Jonathan and Sam did a good job there."

"No need to apologize," Mikaela said with a smile. "I know what you mean. I enjoy it, too. Would you like a drink? Coffee, tea or something cold?"

"If you're having tea, I'll join you. Thank you."

Mikaela rose to find another mug and poured fresh water into the teapot. As she fixed the cup, she asked, "How far did you drive today?"

"Just from Cannebury to here. It usually takes about five hours, but the weather turned just outside of Pemton so we took it slowly. It looks like it's really coming down now."

Mikaela looked out the window to watch the snow falling steadily and the wind picking up to blow it around. "It's the first snowfall of the season. I thought it would melt, but it looks like it's staying."

"I think it'll be up over those chairs by the time it's all said and done," Walt agreed. "When is Sam due home?"

Mikaela looked at the clock. "Soon. He operated today so he shouldn't be too late."

Walt nodded. "They haven't started operating around the clock at this hospital?"

Mikaela shook her heard. "Not yet. They're talking about it, but so far they haven't had the volume to warrant it. Maybe as the population grows? I know Sam would appreciate it. He's always looking for more OR time."

"That's probably the only thing he doesn't like about this new job," his mother agreed.

"Well, it's the bread and butter that pays the bills," Walt said. "It's hard to do your job as an eye surgeon without the surgery."

"So Mikaela, Sam tells us you're a painter."

Mikaela's heart sank. Really? Was that before he knew the whole truth or was that what he wanted his parents to know? She hesitated for a moment, and waged an internal debate. Truth or perpetuating a lie that would be complicated to continue? The truth won. She cleared her throat. "Well actually, I do paint, but it was a business I started with a friend to put myself through university."

"You're an artist?" Marla asked.

"No. It was house painting. It kept us pretty busy in the day."

"What did you take at university?" Walt asked.

"Sciences in undergrad and then medicine. I'm an obstetrician-gynecologist."

Both Marla and Walt did a double take.

"An obstetrician-gynecologist?" Marla asked, stiffening and leaning back in her chair.

Mikaela was taken aback. "S . . . Sam didn't tell you?"

"No, he didn't," Marla said firmly. "I do hope that your profession hasn't turned you away from having children."

"N—No," Mikaela stammered.

"Well, that's a relief," Marla said. "I'm looking forward to having more grandbabies."

Sam's dad sat in stony silence. "Are you any good?"

Mikaela looked at him. That wasn't a question she heard every day. "I think so."

"Humph," Walt grunted. "Not all of them are."

There's a story there, Mikaela thought. "No, not all."

Walt's eyes widened slightly and a glimmer of respect swept his features.

"Well," said Marla with forced cheerfulness, "if you think Sam will be home soon, maybe I'll get dinner ready. That is, if you don't mind eating early."

"No, not at all. That'd be great. I can help. Should I text Sam to see where he is?"

"Well, I don't like to bother him, but it would be helpful. And I suppose if he's busy, he'll just answer when he's free."

Mikaela nodded. "The benefit of texting. I'll go grab my phone."

Without glancing at Walt and uncomfortable with the tension in the air, Mikaela left the room. She could hear Marla speak in a soothing voice and shut the bedroom door to respect their privacy.

Mikaela picked her cell phone off the dresser and sat down heavily on the bed. Sam's parents had seemed so friendly before she corrected them about her job. What was that all about? She thought it would feel good to tell the truth. But it hadn't at all. She rubbed the ache over her heart.

She glanced at her cell phone. Sam had sent a text twenty minutes earlier.

On my way.

He should be home by now. Glancing out the window, Mikaela saw dark clouds and gray skies. Snow piled up and drifts were forming as the wind swirled the snow against the house. As she debated whether to go and shovel the driveway for Sam, the front door opened and Sam shouted hello.

Mikaela took her time joining them to give Sam some time to say hello to his parents. When she walked into the kitchen, they were standing around the island chatting.

Sam glanced over, and reached out to draw her close and drop a gentle kiss on her lips. "So I take it you've met Mikaela," Sam said to his parents as he gave Mikaela a reassuring squeeze.

"We did, indeed," Marla beamed. "We had a nice chat. You've met your match, dear. I see you make a lovely couple together," she said as her expression softened.

Sam smiled. "I knew you'd approve."

"She says she's an obstetrician," Walt said flatly.

Sam looked over at his dad. "Yes."

Mikaela caught the look that passed between the two. She was not going to be the cause of tension between Sam and his dad. "Is that a problem?"

Marla started to fuss. "Of course not—"

"As a matter of fact, it is," Walt said, folding his arms across his chest.

"Why?" Mikaela asked with a frown.

"I don't like obstetricians."

Mikaela studied his face. He was serious. That was a first. She'd had women unhappy with her in the throes of a delivery, but it never lasted. And the partners always seemed happy, even grateful, that someone else was sitting at the other end where the action was happening. "Why?"

Walt just looked at her with sad eyes and a stony expression.

"Dad," Sam began.

"No, I think it would be better if I understood," Mikaela said.

"I don't have any respect for them. They're a bunch of quacks and half the time they don't know what they're doing," Walt said.

"I'm sorry," Mikaela said quietly.

"Sorry? Sorry for what?" Walt asked.

"I'm sorry you feel that way. And I'm sorry if something happened that made you feel that way."

"What do you know about it?" He looked at her sharply.

"Nothing really." Mikaela sighed. "But you're right. Well, partially right. Despite all of our training, we don't always have control over what happens in a delivery. It's sad. As much as I wish for a happy ending every time, it doesn't always happen. It's heartbreaking for everyone."

Walt looked away and stuffed his hands in his pockets. Finally he cleared his throat and looked Mikaela in the eye. "I appreciate your honesty," he said gruffly.

Mikaela nodded without saying anything.

"Well," Marla said, breaking the tension, "let me get the table set for dinner. I've brought fried chicken and potato salad. Are we ready to eat?"

"I am," said Sam. "Let me get changed." He tugged on Mikaela's hand. "Coming?"

Chapter 17

happenstance horoscope

ARIES (March 21-April 19) You'll be touched by the support around you. Take what's offered. Jumping in when needed will bring its rewards. Don't hesitate.

Sam led Mikaela to the bedroom and shut the door behind them. He turned her to face him. "I'm really sorry about that."

Mikaela raised her hand to stop him and shook her head. "Don't apologize, Sam. You're not responsible for your father's words. I didn't want something like that hanging in the air every time we met. Better to air it now and know where we stand."

"Maybe," said Sam. "But I could have warned you. They lost a child," Sam explained. "I don't remember much, and they hardly ever talk about it. I was six years old, and my mom was pregnant. They went to the hospital with my mom in labor, and everything was good but then came home devastated. The baby died at birth. Obviously my dad blames the obstetrician. I don't really know what happened, but there was a lot of anger with the grief. That was my first funeral."

"I'm so sorry, Sam," Mikaela said quietly.

"Thanks. Just give my dad time. It's not personal."

"Of course. I don't want to come between you two. I'm sorry to make him, your mom, and you, relive that grief."

Sam shrugged and shook his head. "You didn't." Sam looked around the room. "Sorry about all this. There's room in the closet for your stuff." He pulled off his tie and unbuttoned his dress shirt as he entered the walk-in closet.

Mikaela swallowed and sat down on the bed. She heard him unbuckle his belt.

"They don't usually stay more than a couple of days," Sam said. He had changed into jeans and walked out into the bedroom shirtless. Grabbing a sweatshirt off the floor, he pulled it over his head.

Enjoying the view, Mikaela sat on the bed and nodded.

Catching her expression, Sam walked over and stood in front of Mikaela. He pulled her to her feet. "We should go back out there."

Mikaela nodded.

"Hungry?" Sam asked softly.

Mikaela nodded.

Sam smiled and bent his head to brush his lips over hers. "Me, too," he whispered.

Mikaela rose to meet him and enjoyed the feel of his hard chest against her. He deepened the kiss and she slipped her hands through his hair.

How many nights had she lain awake wanting this? she thought, pressing closer. She couldn't get enough of his touch. She loved the feel of his lips and his tongue and oh god . . . they should stop . . . his parents were in the next room . . . she was going to have to share a bedroom with him tonight . . . her heart was going to break. She stepped back abruptly.

"Your mom's waiting with dinner. We should go," she said, her voice shaky as she brushed a hand through her hair.

"Sure." Sam tried to read her expression.

Mikaela avoided meeting his eyes. She opened the bedroom door and, straightening her clothes, went to the kitchen. Sam followed behind her more slowly.

Marla was just setting the plates on the table when they walked in.

"I can get the cutlery," Mikaela said, a little too brightly.

"Thank you dear. Then I think we're all set." Marla set the plates out and added serving spoons to the chicken and the salads.

"Would anyone like wine?" Sam asked. "Or a beer? Dad?"

"I'll have a beer if you're having one," Walt replied.

"Yeah, I could use one."

Mikaela sent Sam a guilty glance. She barely had a handle on how to act when they were alone. His parents in the house just added another complicated layer. He caught the look and she quickly looked away.

Mikaela swallowed the last crumb of her pie and wiped the napkin across her lips. "That was delicious, Marla. Thank you very much for bringing dinner," she said as she sat back, feeling pleasantly full.

"Yes. Another outstanding meal, Mom. Thank you. Would you like coffee or tea?" Sam asked, glancing at his parents.

"I'd love an extra-hot, sugar-free, caramel, half-caf, skinny, grande, moche latte with a little extra foam," his mom said.

Sam stopped and stared.

"Just kidding. I've always wanted to order that," she said with a laugh. "A herbal tea would be lovely, dear, if it's not too much trouble."

Sam chuckled. "Tea, I can do."

Mikaela stood up to help.

"Relax. I can get it," Sam offered. Sam collected the plates and brought them to the counter, on his way to filling the kettle and brewing the coffee.

As he set steaming mugs down a few moments later, Sam glanced out the window. "It's a good thing you came today. Look at that snow. It doesn't look like it's slowing down at all."

Gone were the big fluffy snowflakes that drifted down quietly earlier in the day. Now the wind whistled against the windows. As darkness settled, the snow blew in white sheets across the lake, cresting on waves that crashed and roared against the shore.

"If it can't be seen, it wants to be heard," Mikaela murmured.

"I hope you don't have to go out tonight," Marla said with concern.

Mikaela and Sam shook their heads as Mikaela's phone rang. She picked up her phone and wandered to the next room. "Hello?"

"Hello, Dr. Finn. It's the Emerson Hospital switchboard here. Dr. Grant is on the line for you. Please hold." There were a series of clicks. "Go ahead."

"Mikaela?"

"Hi Sylvie. How's it going?"

"Good. Good," she said in a distracted voice. "Sorry to bother you at home. I know you're not on call, but I was wondering if you could take a look at a patient. She's a primip in her thirty-sixth week, followed by Dr. Henderson at St. Peter's. Her contractions started about three hours ago, and the ultrasound shows the baby is breech. With this weather, she's not going to make it to Rivermede and it looks like she's heading toward a C-section. Any chance you're around and could come?"

Mikaela glanced out at the raging storm and grimaced. "Yes, of course. I just need to shovel out from the mess outside, but I could be there in half an hour."

Sylvie sighed in relief. "That would be great."

"If you could make sure she's prepped and ready to go in case it all happens fast, I'll be as quick as I can."

"Great. Thanks. See you shortly."

Mikaela hung up the phone and walked back into the kitchen. "That was the hospital. Unfortunately I have to go in and help out with a delivery."

Marla looked at her sympathetically. "Oh dear. We spoke too soon."

Sam stood up. "I'll grab a shovel and get a path cleared to the road. You can take the Jeep. It has four-wheel drive and will be safer. Hopefully the snowplows have been out this way," he said as he poured the rest of his coffee in the sink.

"I'll help, too," Walt said as he got up and followed Sam.

"I'll just get changed and join you," Mikaela said.

"I can drive you to the hospital, Mikaela, if you're worried about driving," Sam offered. He pulled on boots, tugged on a hat, and found warm gloves.

Mikaela looked at him gratefully. She hated driving in weather. "Really? What about getting back home? If I drive, I can stay the night if the roads are terrible."

Sam shrugged. "I can do some paperwork and wait for you. I could always crash in one of the on call rooms."

She was so relieved she almost wept. "That would be great."

"No problem. Let's see if we can get out of the driveway."

Mikaela went to change and quickly grabbed some overnight essentials. She was pulling on a warm coat and scarf when Sam came back in. Walt followed behind him and stamped the snow off his boots.

"That was fast," Mikaela said with raised eyebrows.

"Turns out you have friends in high places." Sam grinned.

"What?"

"Look," Sam said as he opened the door.

A massive snowplow was slowly backing out of the driveway, clearing a wide swatch as it went.

"What's he doing?"

"Apparently he's the uncle of the newborn you're about to deliver. They got word to him that you needed to get to the hospital pronto, so he's here to deliver you. Not your average limo but considering the weather . . . "

"Much preferred. That's so great."

Sam laughed.

"I better get going. Thanks for offering to drive me. I appreciate it," she said and leaned over and pressed her lips softly to his. "Wish me luck. I'll let you know how it goes, but don't wait up for me." She scooted out the front door, and pushing against the swirling snow, she climbed up into the waiting snowplow.

Mikaela waved as the snowplow honked and slowly pulled out into the road.

Chapter 18

Written in the Stars by Esmeralda Garnet

ARIES (March 21-April 19) Doing a job well will bring its own rewards. Emotional issues demand your attention. Proceed with caution.

Mikaela curled up on the couch in her office and tugged a blanket up over her shoulders. It was three o'clock in the morning, and she was grateful for the break. The patient had ended up needing a Cesarean section, and a healthy six-pound baby boy had been delivered at nine o'clock that evening. The baby was in the neonatal intensive care unit for observation for a few hours as a precaution, and the mom was settled in a room.

Mikaela ended up staying at the hospital to care for two more women in labor who arrived just as she was finishing up the first delivery. One delivered an eight-pound baby girl, but the other looked like she was going to be a while yet. Time to catch a break, Mikaela sighed, and snuggled deeper into the warmth.

She was really growing to love this small town. Where else would they rally together to make sure she arrived safely at the hospital? One of the nurses on the obstetrical floor had called her aunt at the dispatch for the city works. She put the bulletin out that Mikaela needed to get to hospital. The driver hadn't realized his sister-in-law had gone into labor, but he hustled over, as fast as a snowplow could hustle, and cleared the way. It was definitely the way to go in a raging snowstorm. The massive truck plowed through the piles of snow on slippery roads like it was a sunny day. Friends in high places, she chuckled, were definitely a bonus.

Mikaela closed her eyes and tried to relax. She figured she had two, maybe three hours before they called her again. She sent Sam a text and wondered how he made out with his parents. He seemed to enjoy their company, and it actually worked out well that he could spend some time alone with them.

And Mikaela had one more night of reprieve. She couldn't imagine how the night would've gone if she'd stayed home. Well, she could imagine, that was the problem. She shivered at the thought of spending the night with Sam. Just seeing his hot, hard, naked body stopped her brain working. She loved the feel of his skin against her. She loved his lips on hers and loved being held by him. She sighed. She loved him. Period. That sent an ache raging through her. He offered to drive her, made her dinners, and was fun. He made her heart race.

She was toast. When this charade ended, she was going to get burned. Live in the moment, Mikaela told herself. Enjoy each day and the time you spend with Sam. It should be easier for her, knowing it wasn't going last. But it really wasn't. It was like feeding an addiction, knowing that eventually, she was going to have to deal with the problem. But this addiction made her feel really good. So like any other addict, she vowed to deal with it. Tomorrow. She hoped tomorrow never came.

Chapter 19

happenstance horoscope

ARIES (March 21-April 19) Go to a place that nurtures mind, body and spirit. The past plays a role in shaping your future. Be cautious about revealing all you know.

On Friday evening, Mikaela unlocked her condominium door and let herself in. She had chickened out.

Marla and Walt had decided to stay an extra two days so the snow-covered roads would be cleared before they continued their drive down south. The storm had abated over night. The temperatures had dropped and the day had been filled with bright sunshine. The major roads had been cleared of snow but were still slushy and wet as the salt and sand started to work. Mikaela understood why they wanted to delay their drive to Arizona, but the drive to Rivermede was doable. So she made her excuses and did it.

It was better this way, Mikaela reasoned. She wasn't ready to spend the night with Sam. She hadn't been back to her condominium in over a month and needed to check on it. Theoretically.

Mikaela thought she saw a flicker of disappointment in Sam's eyes when she announced she was leaving for the weekend. It boosted her ego for a moment and almost made her change her mind. But in the end, she just didn't want to deal with the situation. She wasn't ready to share Sam's bed. So Mikaela spent Thursday night at the hospital. On Friday after work, she said her good-byes to Sam's parents, smiled through Marla's offer of help with the wedding plans, shook Walt's hand with polite distance, and escaped.

Mikaela tossed her keys on the table and set her overnight bag on the floor. She looked around at the familiar surroundings with the comforting hues of beach sand and seawater, and relaxed. Tension drained from her shoulders, and the fatigue lifted as she removed her coat and boots. She turned up the thermostat and wandered through the living room, snapping on lights, and pulling curtains shut to keep the warmth in as the evening sun set.

Mikaela flipped through the mail, which the neighbor had left lying on the kitchen counter. She sorted out the bills and threw the flyers into the recycling.

She glanced at the clock and realized she had an hour before Margo came over. She had called her to arrange a girls' night in with pizza and a movie, but there was plenty of time to unwind with a long soak in the tub.

She opened a bottle of Margo's favorite red wine, to let it breathe. Luckily she wasn't a wine snob like Margo. Her first glass didn't need to breathe. She carried it upstairs and started the tub running. She shed her clothes and wrapped herself in a warm terry robe. Bath salts in the water filled the air with a sweet vanilla fragrance. Mikaela sat on the edge of the tub and let the warm, almost hot, water cascade through her fingers. She slipped out of her robe and slipped into the bubbles, sinking down to her chin and closing her eyes.

Mikaela was not going to think about lying to Sam's parents about the engagement. She was not going to think about Marla's sweet nature and Walt's silent disapproval. She was not going to think about Sam's hot body and the legions of women who enjoyed it before her. Or her job, the clinic, or the mound of charting she needed to do. For one blessed hour she would just be. Mikaela concentrated on the hot fragrant water, on relaxing every muscle of her body, and just enjoyed having time off.

She needed to let her mind go to her happy place. Her happy place was a beach. Watching kids playing in the sand and teenagers tossing a Frisbee while she floated on the waves in a sparkling blue-green ocean. Hearing laughter and seagulls and waves breaking on the shore. Feeling the sun on her face with a light breeze lifting her hair and smelling the fresh clean air of the ocean mixed with the coconut sweetness of sunscreen. Being outside with nothing more to do than laze on the beach and jump in the waves like a child.

Mikaela stayed at the beach until the water turned tepid and her toes started to wrinkle. But it definitely did the trick. She felt refreshed and in a happier mood as she pulled on sweatpants and a sweatshirt.

She headed to the kitchen to wait for Margo. The doorbell rang as she set down plates and napkins.

"Hello, stranger." Margo smiled when Mikaela answered the door. She held a pizza box off to the side and opened her arm for a hug as she stepped in out of the cold.

Mikaela laughed and held Margo tight. "It's been too long."

Margo handed Mikaela the pizza box and slipped off her coat.

"Meat lovers, I presume," Mikaela said, tongue-in-cheek.

Margo snorted. "As if," she said. "If I got anything other than Hawaiian, you'd make me go back and get another." She hung her coat in the closet.

"And rightly so," Mikaela retorted. "And then I would have to question the whole foundation of our friendship."

"Right. And as such intense scrutiny might not be good for anything, including our minds on our night off, I thought I'd just stick with Hawaiian."

"Good choice," Mikaela agreed amicably.

They grinned at each other and headed to the kitchen.

They sat in the kitchen nook with glasses of wine and thick slices of piping hot pizza. After a few bites and the worst of the hunger settling, Margo looked at Mikaela. "So, I sensed a sort of SOS in your call this afternoon."

Mikaela started to deny it automatically and then fell silent.

Margo picked up her wine glass. "Is everything okay?"

Mikaela sighed. "Compared to the global scene with world hunger and civil war, my life is good." She bit into a slice of pizza and caught a string of melted cheese.

Margo smiled, took a sip of wine, and set her glass down. "But . . ."

"But compared to the average person who is not caught up in half truths and deception . . . mine's a little complicated." Mikaela set the pizza down and wiped her mouth with a napkin.

Margo eyed Mikaela with sympathetic eyes and kept silent.

"I know. I know," Mikaela said, throwing her hands in the air. "You're trying really hard not to say 'I told you so,' and I appreciate your restraint."

Margo feigned innocence and made Mikaela laugh.

"It's slowly spinning out of control and I needed to spend time with someone who knows the whole truth so I don't have to filter what I'm saying." Mikaela leaned back and swirled the wine in her glass.

"Do I? Know the whole truth?" Margo asked.

"Yes, of course. I would never lie to you."

You don't consider them lies, Margo thought silently, but kept quiet. She'd known Mikaela for a long time and understood why Mikaela did what she did and said what she said. She understood it wasn't just selfish carelessness on Mikaela's part. It was partly safety and partly self-preservation. "What happened?" She took a bite of pizza and watched Mikaela's shoulders sag.

"Sam's parents dropped by," Mikaela said. "It's not enough that we're deceiving everyone at work, now his parents have joined the fray. And that," Mikaela said slowly, "was hard. They're staying for a couple more days, and I needed to get away."

"Are they terrible?"

"No, not at all. Which is probably why I'm so affected by it." Mikaela sipped her wine. "Sam's dad has a problem with obstetricians so he's distant, but it's a polite distance. Sam's mom is sweet and interesting and supportive, and I don't want to hurt her."

"You don't want to hurt her or you don't want to be hurt?" Margo asked, raising her eyebrows.

Mikaela was quiet for a while. Margo was getting ready to apologize when Mikaela finally mumbled, "Both."

Margo covered Mikaela's hand with her own. "I'm sorry, sweetie,"

"Thanks," Mikaela said with a sniffle. "It's a mess."

"How does Sam feel?"

"I don't know. We don't talk. I mean, we talk about other stuff but not about us. It's very awkward being engaged but not really being engaged," Mikaela said.

Margo laughed. "That's probably why more people don't do it."

"And smart they are." Mikaela shook her head. "Man, I didn't think it would be this hard to live with someone and not fall in love. If anything it just makes me love him more," she said miserably.

Margo smiled sympathetically and squeezed Mikaela's hand. "He's got the ass factor?"

Mikaela sighed deeply. "A great ass, a bit of sexy, badass attitude, and all of my heart. He's got the ass factor. He's it for me."

"That's so great. You should talk to him. Tell him how you feel."

Mikaela looked appalled. "I don't think so."

"Why not?" Margo tilted her head. "It's called being honest."

"Yeah, honesty in relationships hasn't worked out too well for me. And what happens," Mikaela continued quickly, "if he doesn't love me, and then we have to live in this charade even more awkwardly for the next nine months?"

"Nine months?" Margo jerked and sat up straight. "Are you pregnant?"

"No. NO." Mikaela shook her head emphatically, her eyes wide. "We decided we would stick with this 'engagement,'" she finger quoted in the air, "for a year, three months of which are almost done. We figured by then Sam would be engrained at the hospital, and breaking up wouldn't impact his career."

"And what about yours?" Margo took another bite of pizza.

"Then I could decide if I wanted to stay."

She swallowed her mouthful. "And do you?"

"Want to stay?" Mikaela repeated, fingering the stem of her wine glass.

"Yeah."

Mikaela shrugged. "I love the job. The hospital has been upgraded, and it's a dream to work in. I'm enjoying the patients. The staff is probably the most caring and dedicated I've come across. This past week, in that raging snowstorm, one person called another and before I could get my coat on a snowplow showed up to clear my driveway and take me to the hospital. Can you imagine?"

Margo grinned. "No."

"I know. It's crazy. They look out for one another. I love the sense of community in a small town." Mikaela sighed.

"But . . . "

"But, I love Sam."

Margo's chest tightened when she saw Mikaela's eyes fill. "But that's great, isn't it? Maybe your engagement will become real, and your conscience will be clear."

Mikaela grimaced. "Sure. If Sam loved me back and if he wanted to get married that would be perfect." She rolled the edge of the napkin. "He's had quite the parade of women, apparently, and I'm not sure he wants to settle for just one. Just me." She unrolled the napkin and rolled it again.

"You need to talk to him. Tell him how you feel."

"I can't. What if he doesn't? What if he has no intention of continuing this past one year?" Mikaela raised sad eyes to Margo.

"Well then, you have to let it go and move on," Margo said with a shrug. "But if he does, then it could be the start of something beautiful."

"I'm more worried that if he doesn't, it will be the start of something ugly. And I'll be even unhappier. With nine months left to go sharing a living space." Mikaela took a gulp of wine.

Margo finished the last bite of her pizza and wiped her hands on a napkin. "Has he given you any impression one way or another about how he feels?"

"I don't know. I wondered whether he was disappointed when I left for the weekend, but that could just be my imagination. I think he still wants me," Mikaela said, looking in the distance, a faint flush on her cheeks, "but I don't believe he loves me."

"Wanting you isn't enough?"

"Not without love," Mikaela said quietly.

"I don't like to see you so unhappy," Margo said, shaking her head.

"I know. I'm sorry. I'll straighten it out. I will talk to him." Mikaela moved the napkin to the other side of her plate.

"That's good," Margo encouraged.

"When the year is up, I'll sit down with him and have a heart to heart. My heart," she said with a grimace, "I'm not sure about his."

"But that's nine months away," Margo argued.

"I know. But look how quickly the first three months went by," Mikaela said. "Look, I'm sorry I dragged you into this. I just want to be with you and enjoy an evening when I don't have to think about all this." She waved her glass of wine in the air.

"Well, then, we shall," Margo said with a nod. "We can finish this bottle of wine and the pizza and eat all four of the éclairs I'm hoping are in that box." She pointed to the baker's box on the kitchen table. "We can do whatever you want."

Mikaela reached over and hugged her. "Thanks Margo. You're the best."

Margo squeezed her back and smiled. "I am, aren't I?"

Chapter 20

Zodiac Zach – Don't leave home without him.

ARIES (March 21-April 19) Be strong as others look to you for support. Don't limit what you can do or question your worth because of an emotional situation. You will gain respect through your actions.

Mikaela waited until Monday morning to drive back to Emerson. Her clinic didn't start until nine o'clock in the morning, the forecast was clear so the roads would be dry, and it meant she could avoid any possible awkwardness for another night. Just in case. She knew she was being a chicken, but convinced herself that it was cautious, even wise. Mikaela texted Sam to let him know she wouldn't be back on Sunday night and then spent the night tidying her condominium in case it was another month before she returned.

At seven a.m., Mikaela wrote a quick note of thanks to the neighbor who brought in her mail, lowered the thermostat, and with a sigh of regret, locked the door behind her.

The sun was shining and glistened off the snow-covered trees that lined the highway. Traffic was light and the roads dry, so she cranked up the radio and sang along, out of tune, making the time pass quickly. She drove directly to the hospital and made it there in under an hour.

Mikaela looked forward to the day. She had prenatal clinics booked all day, and with the nurse running two patients ahead of her, it usually went smoothly. There was a good chance the clinic would finish on time, maybe even with a break for lunch.

The day passed quickly. Only one patient left and she could head home to Sam. Mikaela pressed a hand to her stomach to settle the butterflies fluttering at the thought of being alone with Sam again. It had only been four days, but she missed him. He usually had dinner waiting for her on Mondays and she wanted to sit down, share a bottle of wine, and hear about his day.

Would she move back into her own room? Did she want to? She thought fleetingly of his hard body pressed against her and the soft kisses that made her knees go weak. He took her breath away and stole her heart.

But until the butterflies settled, she preferred to keep things as they were. He didn't need to know how he affected her. All she had to do was keep the picture of a naked Sam out of her mind, and she would be fine. She just wished that wasn't getting harder to do.

Mikaela reviewed her notes for the last patient. Joanne Sycamore. Age thirty-six. First pregnancy. Expecting twins. Joanne was thirty-four weeks along and had been coming in every two weeks for prenatal care, usually accompanied by her husband, Rob.

At the most recent visit, one week ago, Mikaela had raised concerns about the size of one of the twins, and Joanne had broken down in tears. She'd lost her twin brother at the age of twelve in a motor vehicle accident.

The brother and sister had been inseparable, and twenty-four years later, Joanne still grieved his death. She had a deep-rooted fear of the same thing happening to her babies and was very particular, almost obsessed, with doing everything she could to ensure a healthy outcome.

Paula, Mikaela's nurse, came out of the examining room. The worried frown on her face was not encouraging. "Her urine screen and blood pressure are fine, but her weight is down two pounds, and I can only get one fetal heartbeat." She pressed her lips together. "Joanne is . . . upset."

Mikaela nodded. "I'll go and examine her. Bring the ultrasound in, and we'll take a quick look. Maybe you should give the OR a heads up, too."

Paula nodded and headed off as Mikaela entered the room.

Joanne looked up with damp eyes. "The nurse said she could only hear one baby's heartbeat. For the last two days, they haven't been as active," she said as she wiped tears from her cheeks. "I thought maybe it was just getting crowded in there. I didn't think to come in." She covered her face with her hands.

"Joanne, try to stay calm," Mikaela put her hand on Joanne's shoulder and spoke in a low voice. "Let me examine you, and we'll do another ultrasound and see what's happening."

Mikaela examined and measured the size of Joanne's uterus and then picked up the Doppler to listen to the heartbeat. She moved the probe from one quadrant to another and caught and counted one fetal heartbeat. It was a strong one hundred and forty-two beats a minute. Mikaela's heart sank as she moved the probe around and heard only silence. Paula knocked on the door and pushed the ultrasound machine in.

"Let's do another ultrasound, Joanne," Mikaela said.

Mikaela set up the screen, adjusted the image, and scanned Joanne's abdomen. She focused on the healthy twin first, measuring its size and noting the strong heartbeat. She paused as she found the second twin. Its size was unchanged from a week ago, and even scanning from a different angle, Mikaela could not see a heart beat. The baby had died in utero.

Mikaela set the probe down and pushed the machine to the side. She wiped the gel from Joanne's abdomen and lowered her gown.

She watched tears stream down Joanne's face, as she looked her in the eye. "I'm so very sorry, Joanne. I can only find one heartbeat. The smaller twin has died."

"No," Joanne cried, covering her ears. "I don't want to hear that. I don't want it to be true. No. No," she pleaded.

Mikaela looked at her helplessly. “I’m sorry.”

Joanne covered her face as she sobbed.

There was a quiet knock on the door, and Paula poked her head in. “Her husband is here.”

Mikaela motioned for her to let him in.

A tall man with a rumpled suit, loosened tie, and harried expression hurried into the room. He glanced at Mikaela and gathered his wife in his arms.

“I’m sorry, Rob, one of the twins has died,” Mikaela said quietly.

“Oh.” Rob sighed heavily and with a look of utter sadness, closed his eyes and kissed the top of his wife’s head. “I’m so sorry, honey,” he whispered.

Joanne buried her head in his shoulder as her small frame wracked with sobs.

“I’ll give you a few minutes alone,” Mikaela said to them.

Rob nodded as he held his wife.

Joanne would need an urgent Cesarean section to deliver the other twin. Mikaela wrote the orders and reviewed the chart. She flipped to the clinic notes from the last visit and, with a frown, wondered why there was no record of the babies’ heart rates. She made a mental note to review the chart more closely after the surgery. More pressing was breaking the news to Joanne about the C-section. The operating room was ready and the pediatric team on hand. Things had to move quickly.

Mikaela pulled off her surgical gown and threw it in the linen hamper. She peeled off her gloves and tossed her mask and surgical cap in the bin outside the surgery. One baby had been sent to the morgue, and the other was in the neonatal intensive care unit. He was six weeks premature but was a good size and had a good prognosis. Joanne was already in recovery with her husband by her side. Mikaela needed to check on her one more time before she left for the evening, but technically everything had gone well.

Wearily, Mikaela sat to write the post-op orders. Just the basics tonight. Tomorrow when she did rounds, she would talk to Joanne about counseling and see what would be helpful. But tonight Joanne needed to rest and start to heal.

It was late and the hospital was quiet as Mikaela made her way to her office. She glanced at the stack of papers in her inbox, but couldn't summon up the energy to go through them. That could wait another day. She shrugged into her coat, tugged on her boots, and made her way slowly to her car.

Sending a tiny little person to the morgue was heartbreaking. It happened, Mikaela knew. Even when they did everything right, with all the technology at their fingertips, it happened. Was it genetics? A virus? She sighed. Shitty luck? Who the hell knew? It didn't make any difference to the mother. Once they felt the flutter of life inside them, the death was devastating. And when she had to write 'development incompatible with life' on the death certificate, her heart broke as well.

Mikaela felt her eyes fill as she pulled into the driveway. She knew she couldn't get wrapped up in it and had managed to hold it together for Joanne and Rob. But now, alone, in the silence of the night, she could shed a tear for the little life that she had to pronounce dead at its birth. She would never get used to it.

Mikaela wiped her eyes, gathered her briefcase, and stepped out of the car. Damn. She had forgotten to text Sam to let him know she'd be late. She had remembered as she closed the incision, but had forgotten again by the time the surgery finished. Sighing, she went inside.

Chapter 21

Written in the Stars by Esmeralda Garnet

ARIES (March 21-April 19) Leaning on others doesn't make you less strong. An unexpected surprise lightens your day. Love is highlighted.

Mikaela hung up her coat, shed her winter boots, and wandered into the kitchen. She peaked under a dish covered with aluminum foil and found lasagna, topped with melted cheese. She could smell the basil and garlic. It was her perfect comfort food. First she would find Sam, apologize for not calling, and change into comfy clothes.

Mikaela poked her head into the family room and found it empty. She wandered down the hall to the study.

Sam was bent over his desk reading and looked up when she came in. "Hi," he said. "You're home late."

"I am. Sorry for not letting you know," she said quietly.

"No problem. There's lasagna, if you haven't eaten."

"Thanks. I haven't. I'm just going to change, and then I'll get it."

Sam saw dark circles under her eyes and traces of tears she hadn't quite managed to wipe away. "Rough day?"

Mikaela shrugged. "Rough ending to the day."

"Come here."

"What?"

"Come here."

Mikaela moved closer, and when Sam held out his hand, she placed hers on his. He gave a tug, and she fell into his lap. She was so surprised she started to get up.

"Relax," Sam whispered.

With a sigh, Mikaela did just that. She closed her eyes, rested her head against his chest, and listened to the steady beat of his heart. He wrapped his arms around her and rubbed her back as the tension of the day melted away.

"Do you want to talk about what happened?" Sam asked after a few minutes.

"A twin died at birth."

Sam hugged her close. "That would be tough."

Mikaela blinked tears away and nodded.

"How's the mom doing?"

"She's not taking it very well. Obviously it was a shock, and then she had to be rushed to the OR to save the other twin. He's in NICU, but he looks good. Technically, the surgery went well."

"And how are you doing?"

She sighed. "I'm okay. Just sad."

"Shit happens. You can be the best doctor out there and do everything you can for the best possible outcome. And still, shit happens."

Mikaela felt a fresh wave of tears and blinked rapidly to stop them from falling. She hugged Sam close. He probably didn't even realize how much his faith in her, what his simple acceptance and understanding, meant to her.

"Thanks," she said, when she could speak again. "I know that. When I look at everything with a critical eye, when I consider all the options and ways this could have been handled, I know in my head that the outcome wouldn't have been different. If anything, the health of the other twin could have been compromised. I know that. But it was such a tiny life. And the family will never be the same." She sat quietly listening to the soothing sound of his heartbeat.

"At first when I looked at the chart I couldn't find vitals from the last visit. But they were there. I've gone over everything in my head, and nothing we could have done would have made a difference. But I'm going to grieve for a time." She closed her eyes and inhaled the earthy scent of his skin.

"I'm here if you need a shoulder to lean on," Sam said as he brushed a lock of hair from her face. "For as long as you need."

Mikaela leaned back and looked at Sam. "Thank you," she whispered and pressed her lips to his.

Sam stirred and deepened the kiss. He pulled back and rested his forehead on hers. "You're welcome. Why don't you go change, and I'll heat up some dinner for you. Mrs. Davy makes a mean lasagna."

"That sounds wonderful."

Sam's hands spanned Mikaela's waist as he lifted her off his lap. The causal brush of his hand against her breast caused Mikaela's heart to skip as she rose unsteadily to her feet. She looked away and hoped he hadn't noticed her reaction.

Mikaela walked into the guest room automatically, but finding the closet empty, remembered her clothes were still in Sam's bedroom. She went to his room, and the tangled sheets and tousled covers made her imagine Sam in bed. Naked. Focus, she chided herself and changed into soft pants and a sweatshirt. Mikaela splashed cool water on her face and ran a brush through her hair. She'd have to deal with her stuff later. Right now she was ravenous.

Sam set a plate of garlic toast beside a bowl of steaming lasagna at the kitchen table. He poured them each a glass of wine and sat down across from her.

"Thank you. This looks lovely."

"My pleasure. Mrs. Davy is a great cook. And her lasagna is a specialty."

Mikaela smiled and dug in, moaning with pleasure at the roasted vegetables, melted cheese, and fresh pasta. "Delicious. Did your parents get off okay?"

"Yep. They left on Sunday afternoon. They were hoping to get a solid five hours of driving in on Sunday, stop for a good night's sleep, and have a longer day today. Just before you came in, I heard from them and all is well."

"That's great. I enjoyed meeting them."

Sam smiled. "They enjoyed meeting you, too. They were sorry you didn't stay the weekend and hoped you didn't leave because of them?"

Mikaela winced. "Well, not directly. What did you tell them?"

"Oh, just that you had stuff to do at your condominium and that you had been working pretty long hours since you got here. You hadn't had a chance to go and check on it until now."

"They were okay with that?"

"Yeah, they were fine. They're pretty easy going. Although, my mom did ask me about the wedding several times. I just deferred to you. I'm sure she'll be in touch," he said with a grin.

"Great." She took a sip of wine. "Does it bother you to lie to them about us?"

Sam shrugged. "I don't know. You never know what the future will hold. How was your weekend?" he asked, changing the subject.

"It was good. Margo came over for pizza and a movie on Friday night, and on Saturday we went out to a little club. A med school classmate is a sax player in a jazz band, and we went to see him. The band was good."

"Sounds like it was busy."

"Just busy enough." She broke a piece of garlic toast in half. "Margo had to work early on Saturday and Sunday so we had early nights. But it was fun to see her again. And I had a chance to clean the condo and deal with the mail. It was . . . productive," she said, wiping garlic butter from her chin. Also a bit lonely without him, she thought, but didn't have the courage to tell him.

Mikaela scooped the last of the lasagna from her plate. "That was delicious," she said, setting down her fork.

"Would you like some more? There's more in the fridge."

"No, I'm full. That feels a lot better."

"Did you eat today?"

"I had lunch, but it seems like forever ago."

Sam nodded. "I have something for you."

Mikaela raised questioning eyebrows when Sam disappeared to the study and returned holding a small bag. He handed it to her.

"Did I miss an occasion?" she said, taking the bag reluctantly.

"It's an unbirthday gift."

Mikaela laughed. "I love unbirthdays!" She opened the bag and slowly pulled out a bobblehead doll. She burst out laughing. "This is great."

"I thought it would be a fitting tribute to you for taking on the headship."

"Sir William Osler as a bobblehead. He's probably rolling over in his grave."

"What? It's an honor. Being a bobblehead is the highest form of flattery."

She took the doll from the package and set it on the table, watching its oversized head bounce agreeably. She had to laugh. "I'll take it to work and put it on my desk. His words 'First, Do No Harm' always run through my head when I'm trying to figure out what to do with a patient. I'll try to aspire to his greatness. Thank you, Sam."

"You're welcome. Maybe some day there'll be a Mikaela Finn bobblehead."

"Something the world could definitely do without."

He laughed. "I was just going to watch a hockey game on TV. Would you like to join me?"

"That would be nice."

They picked up their wine glasses and headed to the sitting room. Sam flicked on the television and sank down on the sofa. He put his feet up and tugged Mikaela's hand, pulling her down beside him. Mikaela sighed and curled up beside him, tucking her feet up under her, and resting her head on his shoulder.

Sam kept his arm around her and rested his cheek on her hair. He missed her the last few days. He missed sharing meals and sharing the ups and downs of their day. When she didn't come home for dinner and didn't text, he had a moment. He hadn't been absolutely sure she would come back at all. It had hit home that she really didn't need to. She could live in Rivermede and commute. No one would be the wiser, and their 'engagement' wouldn't be compromised. But it didn't sit well with him at all.

At the start, he was sure they would tire of each other and the charade. It was a means to an end, full stop.

It may have started that way, but slowly, over the last month, the 'end' had changed. He wasn't looking to keep up appearances for his job. The job was fine, but he was still frustrated and disappointed with the operating time. What he had with Mikaela was the opposite. He enjoyed her company and couldn't wait to see her at the end of the day. For the first time, he actually thought about settling down, making the engagement real, and spending his life with one woman.

Funny how the idea of spending the rest of his life with one woman never even entered his airspace in the past. Now, the notion of Mikaela not wanting to be in his life squeezed his chest in a vice grip. He was pretty sure Mikaela didn't think of him as husband material, and he could hardly blame her. Hell, he didn't think of himself as husband material, until just recently. But, he had to admit, when he heard her car drive up, it was a wave of relief that gripped his gut and had him closing his eyes and taking a deep breath of reprieve.

Sam figured he had to take it slowly, for both their sakes, but in his mind, there was a definite shift toward a new goal.

"Who's playing?" Mikaela asked drowsily.

"Boston and Chicago," Sam replied.

"Which team is which?"

"Boston is black and gold. Chicago is red and white."

"Hmmm. Which team are you rooting for?"

"Uh. I'm not a die-hard fan of either. Probably Boston though."

"Oh, okay then. Me, too. Go black and gold."

Sam chuckled. A few minutes later, he listened to Mikaela's steady breathing and looked down to see her features relaxed in sleep. Long lashes brushed her cheeks. Gently stroking the dark circles under her eyes, he thought how lovely she was. She was flourishing in her new role. She had taken to it like a duck to water and seemed to enjoy the different aspects of her job — the clinical work, administrative responsibilities, the meetings. He heard snippets of conversation about her around the hospital about her knack for soothing ruffled feathers, her energy. They loved the new design and her unique ideas. She was positive, never said no, always listened.

Mikaela had found her niche and Sam envied her that. He wished this move had gone that way for him and tried to blow away the disappointment. He should have known it wouldn't be an easy path when it was so difficult to get there. Despite putting pressure on his department head, getting more operating time didn't look promising.

He needed to operate, not only for his patients' sake, but to keep his skills sharp. He picked up extra days here and there, and so far that was working. But it was tedious to cancel a clinic full of patients every time he grabbed a half-day of operating time. It wasn't fair to patients, especially when they were bumped to a new day. Some were starting to complain, and he didn't blame them. So yeah, that end had been disappointing. He hoped the hardest part was behind him.

Sam sat quietly, enjoying the feel of Mikaela in his arms. She was warm and soft and slept quietly. She wouldn't have stayed cuddled so close for so long if she had been awake. She was still tentative with him, especially if he tried to get close.

The game finished so Sam switched off the set. Mikaela didn't stir. He twisted around, and hooking his arm under her legs, he carried her to his bedroom. He set her gently down and covered her with a warm comforter, tucking the edges around her. He looked at her for a long time before getting ready for bed himself.

Chapter 22

happenstance horoscope

ARIES (March 21-April 19) Be realistic when assessing a personal situation, even if it disappoints you. You cannot move forward with confidence without understanding where you have come from.

Mikaela woke slowly and for a moment wondered where she was. She couldn't recall getting into bed, but she was definitely in Sam's bed. The room was still dark, and she quickly glanced at the clock. Seven thirty. There were still a few minutes before she had to get up. Relieved, she relaxed again and felt Sam's side of the bed. It was cold, and she wondered if he had slept beside her. She looked at the rumpled covers and imprint in the pillow. Maybe. Possibly. Would she have slept through that? No, probably not. She had been dead tired, but she couldn't imagine getting a restful sleep with Sam right beside her. Even now her body tingled at the thought.

Sam was an early riser and most days left the house by this time. So it wasn't surprising that she didn't hear any sign of him now. She flicked on Sam's radio and snuggled under the covers listening to the news and weather as she slowly woke up. She smelled Sam in the covers and snuggled deeper. It was bright, sunny, and cold outside with the usual mix of mayhem and murder around the world. Palent stocks were up, which was good for her father, she thought with a grin.

Thinking of her parents, she mentally added calling them to her list of things to do. She hadn't spoken to them in a while.

She was procrastinating because she knew her mom wanted her to visit over Christmas and bring Sam. Mikaela wasn't sure if Sam was ready for that; or, for that matter, if she was.

Sam's not Elliott, she could hear Margo say. And Mikaela knew that. She was mostly over that lying, cheating, two-timing, scheming bastard. Mostly, she thought, as she took a calming breath and forced herself to relax. He really wasn't worth the effort of any emotion.

Mikaela could admit that now. But it took three years of a busy residency and Margo, thank god for Margo, to get to that point.

At one time, Elliott had been the center of her world. She hadn't been looking for love. In fact, she had been very content to immerse herself in medicine. She was busy with school and had just started her clerkship in the hospital. On one of her very few weekends off, she had gone home to attend a party hosted by her dad's company. Party probably wasn't the right word. Soiree. Yes, soiree was better. Tuxedos, ball gowns, champagne, an exquisite five-course meal in a high-ceilinged, crystal-chandeliered ballroom. It wasn't really her thing. She would have preferred pizza in sweat pants, but this was her parents. She had gone because it had been important to them.

The evening was a celebration and a thank you to the executive, the engineers and the chemists, the Palentologists as they called themselves, who worked tirelessly on the innovative technology to springboard Palent to another level of success.

They had just patented a new polymer that stabilized chemical bonds at temperature extremes. It could be added to plastics and metals and prevented the contraction and expansion caused by high heat or freezing. It was the culmination of three years of intensive research shrouded in the highest level of security. Palent had signed lucrative contracts with multiple manufacturers who intended to incorporate the polymer into microprocessors in electronics and metal in building materials. In the future they had plans to add it to currency around the world. It had the potential to change the world of engineering. The biggest and latest coup was the contract with NASA and the international space station. There was a lot of backslapping and jovial handshaking on their success.

Mikaela couldn't say she understood it completely, despite her father's best efforts to steer her toward the company. She was relieved when her parents accepted her need to study medicine and pursue an application of science in a different way. So, growing up, she listened to the talk of the company's struggles and successes around the dinner table, but she wasn't integral to its success. Which is where Elliott miscalculated, the rat.

He was at the party/soiree. Looking debonair in his tuxedo with his dark hair, dark eyes, and unsmiling sexy seriousness. He wasn't particularly charming or witty. He didn't have a sense of humor or empathy for other people. In fact, she wondered now, what she had ever seen in him at all. Tall, dark, faintly mysterious. Is that what appealed to her? She shook her head at her naiveté and thanked the stars above that fate had intervened. She shuddered at how close she had come to marrying him, binding her for life, she thought with horror.

She had gone back to school and he had called and pursued her. At first she was flattered and then swept up in the romance of it. Not that he was particularly romantic. He brooded and was soulful. She was a nurturer and his soul mate, he said. He was quiet and moved like a sloth. She enjoyed the quiet after the frantic pace in the hospital, and she found his slow pace restful. And above all this, he needed her.

Oh boy, she had that right, just not how she imagined. He needed her money and her connection to her father's company. In the end she learned he didn't actually need *her*.

Sign these papers, he had said. Just stuff for the wedding. She had believed him. She had trusted him. She probably wouldn't have even noticed, except for Margo. He had thrown the stash of papers among the charts she had brought home to sign. She probably would have just added her signature to those as well. Without a second thought. But Margo had been over and something had caught her eye as she waited for Mikaela to get ready to go out that evening.

"You're going to sign that?" she asked incredulously. "He's *asking* you to sign that?" she said even more strongly.

"What? He said it was paperwork for the wedding or honeymoon or something," Mikaela said vaguely, waving it away.

"It restricts how much you work," Margo said. "And if I read it correctly, that mumbo jumbo speaks to the lineage of your dad's company."

"What? Don't be ridiculous," Mikaela said with a scoff. "Elliott would never make me sign something like that."

Margo just looked at her silently and pointed.

Mikaela sat down heavily in the kitchen chair and scanned the papers. Her eyes blurred when she read the phrase Margo pointed out. She looked up at Margo with shocked eyes. "He's dictating how many hours I spend in medicine? What does all this mean? He expects me to have a role in my father's company, and he expects my share of the company to be controlled by him?" Mikaela read in disbelief. "This is insane."

Margo came over and squeezed Mikaela tightly. "I'm sorry."

Mikaela sniffed and wiped her eyes. "Shit. I would have signed it, too. That's the scary part." She shuddered.

Margo looked at her sympathetically. "Do you have a lawyer who could read it over and explain it to you? Someone you trust?"

"Yes, I can ask Michael." Michael was the head of the legal team at Palent and had worked with her father for years. "He'd probably even look at it today for me."

Michael looked it over and confirmed the worse. It was a prenup that exercised control over pretty much everything she did and owned. Even Michael was a bit shocked at the breadth of the demands.

Needless to say, Mikaela didn't sign it. With barely controlled fury, she returned it to Elliott. Actually she might have thrown it at him. And slammed the door in his face. And then, she wasted tears on him. That was the only thing she regretted.

But she did have one thing to thank Elliott for – he taught her self-preservation. From then on, she was careful in relationships. She guarded her identity, didn't mention her father, and used her mom's maiden name as her own.

She was not going to be used for her money, her family, or her connection to Palent. Only a handful of people knew she was an heiress to a billionaire's fortune. It wasn't how Mikaela identified herself, and she didn't want others to define her that way either.

Mikaela sighed. She wasn't sure Sam was ready for all that. She loved Sam. It caused her heart to ache at the thought of it. But it wasn't enough. She needed him to love her.

Sam was so much better than Elliott. Sam was charming, thoughtful, and romantic. He made her laugh.

How did Sam see her in her job? Granted it was a bit of a rocky start, and he had had to reevaluate that once already. She knew, in her heart, that it was crazy to compare him to Elliott. But it had shocked her that the man she would have taken as her husband, her mate for life, would have thought that she was just dabbling in medicine and wouldn't acknowledge how important it was to her. Sam wouldn't do that, would he? Would he consider his job more important than hers? She cringed as she thought about the move to Emerson. But he saw them as equals? He respected her. Right?

Mikaela groaned. Why does she even worry about this stuff? Because once bitten, twice shy.

So she put off calling her parents until she had time to sort it all out.

Mikaela glanced at the clock. Which wasn't now. She threw back the covers and dashed to the shower to start her day.

Chapter 23

Written in the Stars by Esmeralda Garnet

ARIES (March 21-April 19) A partnership will benefit from your innovative ideas. Look forward to change. You cannot control every situation. Do the best you can for a positive outcome.

Mikaela caught a twenty-minute break at lunch. She spent it multitasking in her office, sifting through paperwork, scanning mail, taking a quick peak at her horoscopes, and eating a tuna lettuce wrap with her third cup of coffee.

There was a memo from one of the hospital engineers with a question about the last room they were finishing. She made a mental note to give him a call.

She wrote a referral for counseling for Joanne and Rob and saw that the autopsy request had been approved but not completed. She sighed as she finished the note.

Physically, Joanne was doing well and had been discharged from hospital. Mentally, she was holding it together and recognized that she hadn't dealt with her twin's death. She wanted to be strong for her baby. It helped that her son was doing really well. He would probably stay in the neonatal intensive care unit for a week or two until he gained a bit of weight, but the pediatricians didn't see any complications arising from his prematurity. So it was hopeful that the family could work toward recovery and have some peace. The funeral was scheduled for the end of the week, so Mikaela made a note to have her schedule cleared so she could attend.

Mikaela flipped to a letter from an ob-gyn resident, in her final year, interested in starting a practice in July. Mikaela scanned the letter quickly, and then sat back and read it through more slowly a second time. The resident was hoping to settle in Emerson. She had family nearby, and although her training was done in a large center, she wanted to return and live in a rural setting. She was open to completing further training in a subspecialty and would be equally happy settling into a general practice. Mikaela scanned her curriculum vitae and the impressive letters of reference that were included. The resident managed to convey enthusiasm for change, which impressed Mikaela, but balanced it with a friendliness that was so inherent in the small community of Emerson.

Mikaela had been toying with the idea of building the department. There'd certainly be enough patients and she had operating time to spare. It was busy enough operating one day a week. Between pre-op, post-op and prenatal clinic visits, and all the surgeries and deliveries they generated, her days were full. She gave away the operating time she didn't need and other departments snapped it up, but the fact she wasn't using it was tracked. At some point, she wanted a partner so she could take holidays and days off, and then, the extra day would be essential.

Mikaela set the letter aside thoughtfully. The timing might be perfect. In six months, the renovations would be complete, and the new delivery suites would be up and running. She could look at office space and staff and create a business proposal to make sure it made sense financially. At the very least, she could set up a meeting with the resident in the New Year and give some thought as to whether a subspecialty would be useful. It would be worth a second look.

Change, Mikaela thought. No fear, no anxiety, no shuddering – just a pleasant positive sensation. She had to smile.

Mikaela had three patients left to see in her afternoon clinic when she received a text from Sam.

Going out to play poker with the boys tonight. Won't be home for dinner.

With a sense of relief, Mikaela texted back.

OK thanks for letting me know. Try not to lose your shirt.

Haha don't wait up.

Mikaela smiled and put her phone away. She gave Sir Osler, now sitting on her desk, a little flip to get him nodding, and it made her laugh.

Her next patient was Nancy Duncan, a thirty-three year old who looked twenty years older than her age. This was her third pregnancy but the first she was keeping. Mikaela had yet to determine if that was because it was so late when Nancy realized she was pregnant or if she actually wanted the baby. Since the referral had been made, Nancy had shown up for only two appointments. Nancy smoked, possibly used alcohol, and swore she was off the cocaine. Mikaela considered it a small victory to have her there.

After checking the nurse's notes, Mikaela walked into the examining room. Blood pressure and urine screen normal. Weight gain fine. The baby was small for its age, but the fetal heart rate was perfect. The pregnancy seemed to be progressing as well as expected, except, Mikaela thought as she looked up, for Nancy's black eye.

"Hi Nancy. How are things going?" Mikaela asked.

"Pretty good, Doctor. Pretty good," Nancy said as she rubbed her palms down her jeans and picked imaginary lint off her sleeve. Her eyes darted around the room.

"Any pain? Any bleeding, at all?" Mikaela asked.

"Um. A little bleeding. For the last few days I noticed blood. Not so much as when I have my monthly, but enough I have to use something," she said looking down at the floor.

"Any cramps with that, Nancy?" Mikaela tried to catch her eye.

"No, no cramps. Just the bleeding." Nancy continued to focus on the floor.

"Let me just examine you." As Mikaela exposed Nancy's belly, she asked, "How have you been feeling otherwise?" Mikaela ran her hands over Nancy abdomen feeling the baby and noticing the faint bruising in the flank. She rattled off a list of questions, but other than a poor appetite, Nancy seemed well.

Mikaela covered Nancy and helped her to sit up. "Come have a seat over here," she directed and held out a hand to help Nancy off the examining table.

Nancy sat down and Mikaela took a seat opposite her.

"You have a black eye and some bruising on your abdomen," Mikaela said quietly.

Nancy sat with her eyes downcast and didn't say a word.

"Do you want to tell me what happened?"

"I . . . I'm just clumsy. I . . . I fell on the stairs."

Mikaela nodded.

"I swear I'll be more careful. It won't happen again. I just wanted to check about the bleeding. It's nothin' wrong with the baby, is it?"

"The heartbeat is strong, but I think we need to do an ultrasound to take a closer look. I'm glad you came in. It was the right thing to do."

Nancy nodded.

"Who's living at home with you now, Nancy?"

"Just me and Jimmy."

"He's the father?"

"Yes."

"How does he feel about the baby?"

"He's okay. Mostly. Doesn't say too much about it. He's not too happy with the weight gain, but it only seems to bother him if he's using."

"What's he using?"

"Weed, hash, coke. Whatever he can get his hands on. But I'm clean. Not touched the stuff since they told me the baby gets it, too."

"That's good, Nancy. Because that's true." Mikaela paused. "Did Jimmy give you the black eye?"

Mikaela watched as emotion shattered Nancy. Shock, shame, and fear flashed in tired eyes and sagged an already weary body.

"Pregnancy is sometimes really hard. It's supposed to be an exciting, joyous time with a new baby on the way, but it can also be scary and stressful." Mikaela paused. "Nancy, if Jimmy is hitting you, I want you to know that you can talk to me about it. There are things you can do and ways we can keep you and the baby safe."

"But I'm clumsy and fat," she sniffled. "I deserve it."

"No, Nancy, you don't. You're not fat. You're pregnant. And no one has the right to hit you."

Nancy just stared with tears rolling down her face. "Where would I go? What would I do? He'd follow me and beat me more for telling someone."

"There's a shelter for women. You could go there and be safe. You could also go to the police for help."

"But he's on probation, and they'll put him back in jail."

"Maybe. But your first concern should be your safety and that of the baby."

"He's so sorry. He promised me he wouldn't do it again," she said wiping her eyes. "I don't want to get him in trouble. I love him."

Mikaela sighed inwardly and wondered if she needed to admit her. "Has he done this before?"

"No, never. And I swear, he said he wouldn't do it again. I believe him." She looked up with a glint in her eye.

Mikaela considered. Her hands were tied if Nancy didn't want to press charges. But she'd need to keep a close eye. "Let's get the ultrasound done. I'd like you to come in every week now. Could you do that?"

Nancy nodded.

"Do you want the number for the shelter?"

"No, Jimmy wouldn't like it if he found it."

Mikaela sighed again. "Remember you can always call the police or go to the Emergency Department if you're scared."

"Okay. Thank you, Doctor."

For what? Mikaela thought. It's not enough. "You're welcome," she said out loud.

Mikaela saw the last two patients of the day, and as she finished her note, Paula came in to tidy up the room.

Paula bustled about with the same energy she had when she started the day. "That's it for today. It was a busy clinic."

"Yes, it's not too late, but already pitch black outside."

"That's the hardest thing about winter," Paula said. "Makes me think I should be hunkering down in hibernation."

Mikaela felt the energy radiating off of her and laughed. "I can't imagine you being anything but active."

Paula laughed with her. "You're right, of course. Makes me think I should be hunkering down, but only briefly. Tonight I'm headed over to the school for badminton."

"Sounds like fun."

"It is. Twice a week for all ages and skill levels. It's fun and a great way to meet people. Keeps me in with the young crowd," she said with a wink. She folded the tape measure and recapped the Doppler gel.

"You go girl! I, on the other hand, am looking forward to hunkering down. A good book by a roaring fire is all I have the energy for."

"That sounds lovely, too. Enjoy your evening." She waved as she headed out to the next room.

Mikaela finished her note and after shutting down the computer, went to her office. She dealt with everything in her inbox. She pulled on her coat and gloves, hooked her briefcase over her shoulder, and locked her office door.

The air was cold and crisp as Mikaela walked to her car. The roads were clear and pulling into the driveway, she saw the full moon just above the house. Making her way to the front door, she stopped to gaze at the stars. Not a cloud in the sky and a dazzling display of twinkling lights. Without the lights of the city, there were dozens more visible. Mikaela could pick out the Big and Little Dippers and follow her way to the North Star, but after that she could only guess. Probably an app for that, she thought. Wouldn't it be lovely to float on her back in the pool and star gaze through the glass? Her stomach grumbled. First, something to eat and then she would head to the pool.

Chapter 24

Zodiac Zach – Don't leave home without him.

ARIES (March 21-April 19) Pay back your debts in a timely manner. A romantic encounter will relieve stress and deepen the bond with someone special. You have more in common than you think.

Mikaela was glad she had taken the time to eat and relax because at ten o'clock that night her pager went off, and she was back at the hospital. The obstetrical suite was hopping all night, and she didn't have a chance to catch her breath until noon the next day. With no clinics booked, she packed her briefcase and thankful for the short drive, headed home.

She dropped her briefcase at the door. Her feet felt like lead and staying upright with her eyes open was a challenge. She stopped at the guest room door, but the bed wasn't made up, and she didn't have the energy to do it. She shuffled down to Sam's bedroom and debated only a moment. Sam was at work, and she craved a soft bed with a warm duvet. Mikaela stripped off her clothes and grabbed one of Sam's T-shirts from the floor. She pulled it over her head and crawled into bed. Snuggling under the covers, she fell asleep with a sigh.

Mikaela was just surfacing from a deep sleep when the door opened quietly. She watched Sam drop a towel from around his waist and pull on a pair of jeans. He looked around the floor for a shirt.

"Hi," Mikaela said softly.

"Hi," Sam smiled. "Sorry, did I wake you? I'll just grab my clothes and let you sleep some more."

"That's okay. I should probably get up anyway or I won't sleep tonight. What time is it?"

"About six o'clock. Did you have a busy night?"

"Four deliveries." Mikaela covered her mouth as she yawned. "One had pre-eclampsia so we had to watch her pretty closely. And one of my patients came in this morning so I didn't get home 'til about noon."

Sam came and sat on the edge of the bed. He brushed hair from her eyes. "Sounds crazy. You don't want to sleep longer?"

"No. I slept pretty soundly this afternoon, so I feel pretty good. I'll get up and have something to eat."

"I can help with that. How do chicken wraps sound? I was just going to make some with the leftover chicken in the refrigerator."

"Chicken wraps sound wonderful. You were just going to whip that up, were you?" She smiled.

He laughed and stood up. "I was. A little leftover magic. I'll grab a shirt and get started. Take your time getting up."

Mikaela's heart melted. She looked from his smiling eyes to the broad shoulders, strong arms, and naked chest. "I borrowed your shirt," she said.

Sam turned and smiled.

"I suppose you'd like it back," Mikaela said. She sat up and slowly pulled the shirt over her head. Her breasts felt heavy and her nipples hardened.

Sam's gaze swept from the shy smile in her sleepy eyes to the creamy fullness of her breasts and back again. "I would like it back," he managed as he stepped up to her.

Mikaela held out his shirt, but didn't let go when he reached for it. She tugged him closer and reaching up to run her hand in his hair, pressed against his naked chest, and kissed him on the mouth. Sam deepened the kiss as they tumbled back onto the bed. Mikaela scraped her nails down his back and wrapped her legs around him.

"You're so warm and soft," Sam said as he trailed kisses down her neck and ran his tongue over soft flesh.

Mikaela moaned as shivers ran down her back. She wiggled closer, running her hands across smooth shoulders and arching up for more. Busy fingers had her spiraling up and frantic, she pushed Sam on his back and straddled him. She took him in slowly and deeply and felt her body swell as he filled her. Pressure in just the right spot, she thought with a moan as he moved inside. The feel of his tongue on her breasts and his hands spanning her waist had her riding faster until she exploded with sensation. Sam tumbled with her and spent, gathered her in his arms and held tight.

Mikaela lay with her head on Sam's shoulder and listened to his heartbeat as it slowed. "Thank you for letting me wear your shirt," she said and smiled.

"Anytime, sweetheart, anytime." Sam chuckled.

Mikaela turned her head and softly kissed Sam's neck. Sam hardened and ran a feather light touch from her breast to the smooth curve of her thigh. She held her breath as his fingers found her core and sensation built again.

"You hungry?" he asked.

"I can wait," she managed.

Sam chuckled. "In that case . . ." he started and flipped her on her back.

Two hours later, Sam and Mikaela sat at the kitchen table eating chicken wraps, listening to the fire crackle and pop in the fireplace. Mikaela pulled her terry robe closer around her and enjoying the flavor combination of hummus, avocado, and spicy chicken, eyed Sam. "That shirt looks better on me," she said casually.

Sam grinned. "I'd have to agree. Personally, I like what you have on under that robe now."

"I'm not wearing anything under this robe."

"Exactly," he smiled and was surprised to see a faint flush on her cheeks.

Charmed, he leaned in. "You take my breath away," he said, catching her gaze and holding it. "And if there's anything of mine you'd like to borrow, you go right ahead. I love the return policy," he said as he bit into the wrap.

Mikaela laughed. "How was work today?"

"It was good. Busy, but there's a good rhythm to the clinic. There's a new young tech assigned to the eye clinic. I can see two patients for every one of hers. Eventually she'll get up to speed, but in the meantime, it creates a bottleneck. Luckily no one seems to mind if I grab an extra chart or two. Today, however, I had the experienced tech who's been there for years. What a difference. If something needed doing, it was done before I wrote the order. The patients were screened and waiting and I was moving at a fair clip. Just goes to show how efficient it could be."

"Sounds more hectic, though."

"Not really. I'd rather be busy and efficient than sitting around cooling my heels, waiting for patients to be put in the lanes."

Mikaela nodded. "It's a strange system at the hospital when departments don't have control over which technicians are hired. It's all about seniority and who can bump who."

"I think that's part of the problem with this new tech. I'm not sure the eye clinic is really what she wanted, but the hours and salary were better than any other option, so she's giving it a go. And sadly, the other applicant for the job was better qualified and more interested."

"Just not as senior," Mikaela added.

"Exactly."

"And the one who is better qualified and more interested will probably end up in labor and delivery," Mikaela said sardonically.

"Probably. But the patients will get a very thorough eye exam." Sam laughed. "Your call is crazy. Have you ever had enough? Especially when you have to go in when you're not on call?"

Mikaela looked at him, trying to gauge what was behind the question. Was he bothered by the time she spent at work? Every man is not Elliott, she chided herself. "No," she said slowly. "It's part of the specialty. Babies come when they come. We can predict all we want, but Mother Nature has the upper hand. And I like the unpredictability. It's part of what attracted me to obstetrics. It's pretty amazing watching nature unfold."

"With two minutes of sheer terror when that newborn pops out," Sam shuddered.

Mikaela laughed. "This from the surgeon who operates within millimeters of the brain. I'll take the newborn."

"I'll stick with the eyeball."

Mikaela finished the last sip of wine as Sam collected the plates.

"You up for a swim?" he asked as he loaded the dishwasher.

"That sounds great. Just let me get a swimsuit on," Mikaela said, getting up from the table.

Sam walked over to stand in front of her. He undid her belt slowly, holding her gaze and slid his hands up her sides, caressing the warm soft skin, barely brushing her breasts.

Mikaela's skin tingled all the way to her toes.

"Can I convince you that you don't need a swimsuit?" Sam whispered as he touched his lips softly to hers and ran kisses along her jawline.

Mikaela closed her eyes, tilted her head to expose her neck and arched her back at the tickle of the teasing lightness. Sam kept his touch barely there as he skimmed over flesh from the smooth curve of her neck to the flat planes of her belly.

Sam slipped the robe from her shoulders. Mikaela found the snap of his jeans and lowered the zipper. She pulled his

T-shirt over his head and ran her hands down the rippling muscles of his abdomen lowering the jeans as she went.

When she trembled, Sam scooped her up. Mikaela wound her arms around his neck.

"The water will be warm," he said as he carried her to the pool, "And I've a need to see you slick and wet."

Much later, Mikaela was wrapped in Sam's arms as they curled together on the bed under a warm comforter. She listened to his steady quiet breathing and tried not to worry.

Look at all the positives. The sex was a huge positive, she grinned. She loved him and she was pretty sure he had feelings for her. Coming home at night and being with him, talking, laughing, she never wanted it to end. And, the sex, well all he had to do was touch her and she melted. She really liked melting.

So why hadn't she told him about her family? Should she worry about his comments about her work and all the time she spent there? Or was she just reading too much into everything he said? she asked herself tiredly.

Their relationship was definitely changing. Mikaela swallowed the panic at the thought of change. Change could be good. Look how it worked out for her job. Change had been the best thing. She found a job she was good at, that was challenging and stimulating. She worked with a great group of people whom she admired and respected. Change was good.

So why did it make her sad? What was it about the two of them together that created a frisson of doubt? Maybe she was more affected by what happened with Elliott than she realized. Was she really still carrying around baggage that she should let go? It wasn't that easy.

She had loved Elliott, in a way. Well, she thought she had loved him. She definitely trusted him, and it still shocked her to have been so completely wrong about him. What if she was reading Sam wrong? What if this was all just a passing fling so he could get what he wanted? It was Elliott all over again. Mikaela silently wiped away a tear. Had she really put herself into that situation again? She sighed. She didn't know and wasn't even sure how to figure it out. Mikaela wished she could just live in the moment and enjoy the ride. But who was she kidding? She needed more. She loved Sam and change was happening. She just needed to decide which was scarier – if he loved her back or if he didn't.

Chapter 25

happenstance horoscope

ARIES (March 21-April 19) Weigh the pros and cons before you make a change. Don't feel pressured to accept something that doesn't feel right. Let others acknowledge what you do and look for greater security.

At five thirty the next evening, Mikaela rolled her shoulders tiredly, shrugged out of her lab coat, and hung it on the hook on the back of her office door. She still had a couple of charts to dictate, but she also had a meeting with Dr. Crispin, the chief of surgery, and didn't want to be late.

His secretary had contacted hers the week before to set up the meeting, and between her schedule and his, this was the first convenient time. Her three-month anniversary at Emerson was coming up, and she wondered if the meeting was a performance review. It was standard procedure, and she didn't expect any surprises.

She made her way to his office and knocked on the door that was standing ajar.

"Come in," he called.

She pushed open the door and saw him standing at a coffee machine. He was a tall man, with a lean face and gray hair at his temples. Mikaela had met with him twice, and had only seen his serious side. She was beginning to think that was the only side he had.

He turned to greet her. "Hello, Mikaela. Come in. I was just getting a coffee. Would you like one?"

Mikaela's heart sank. She had hoped for a quick, perfunctory performance review, so she could head home and have dinner with Sam. If he was settling in with a coffee, it didn't bode well. "Not for me, thanks."

"Take a seat," he invited. He picked up the steaming cup and took a sip as he sat behind a large desk opposite to her. The wall behind him held stacks of books and papers.

He cleared papers from the center of his desk and taking another sip, he moved a folder in front of him. He cleared his throat. "So it's been just over three months since you started here at Emerson. How are you finding it?"

"It's good," she replied. "I'm enjoying the patients and the new clinic. The renovations to the maternity ward are almost complete, and I'm happy with how it's turned out. The transition to the new space has gone smoothly. The nurses and admin staff are great, and I'm really enjoying the sense of community from Emerson."

Dr. Crispin nodded. "Emerson has the feel of a smaller community hospital with the expertise of a bigger center. We're very lucky that way. I think people enjoy your leadership style. You've managed to accomplish a lot, manage a lot of change, and keep everyone happy. I wanted to commend you for that. It's not always easy to satisfy everyone."

"Thank you," Mikaela murmured, pleased and grateful for the feedback.

He shuffled papers in the folder and pulled out a sheet. "I wanted to talk to you, in particular, about the operating room time."

Mikaela looked at him. "Is there a problem?"

"Depends where you're sitting," he said. "Operating time is always at a premium, and some departments are never satisfied. Well, maybe that's too harsh," he admitted. "But they would be happier with more and make that known with regularity. Granted, some specialties, like orthopedics, who are often operating after hours, or ophthalmology, where the demand is greatest, make the most noise. Their waiting lists are long, and the government is looking at ways to cut that back. Bonuses, incentives, penalties, any way you look at it, they want those wait lists cut. And of course, for the hospital board, the bottom line is the dollar. Utilization. Keep costs down, revenues up, maximize resources, I'm sure you've heard it all before."

He adjusted the folder. "We keep track of operating room use. Your trend is approximately seventy-four percent departmental utilization. What you've released, other departments have picked up, so the overall utilization is there, but it's been flagged. Ophthalmology has picked up ninety percent of the days and orthopedics the other ten percent." He cleared his throat. "The request has been made to redistribute the time, to maximize utilization, and to make it more equitable between departments. Now that we've seen what you've used in the last three months, we can make a better projection of what is actually needed. I'm sure you understand." He closed the folder and smiled.

"I'm not sure that I do," Mikaela admitted. "What exactly does this mean?"

"Well, essentially, what we're proposing is that you would keep two units and reassign the other two units to ophthalmology."

"Reassign to ophthalmology?"

"Yes." He shuffled more papers on his desk. "Currently their utilization is one hundred and twenty-two percent of their time. Their need for extra time is greatest," he said, checking the figures in the piles of papers. "It's all just a matter of numbers, really," he said dismissively. "Of course, this would start with the next block of OR."

"And how fluid is this? If my department's needs increase, will the time come back to ob-gyn?"

"Well, theoretically . . ." Dr. Crispin hesitated. "But again, we would have to look at the numbers in each department and see how that would work out most equitably."

"So in a nutshell, no."

He nodded reluctantly. "It would be unlikely, unless there was a real need shown, or the government put incentives in place to justify it."

"And the government has put incentives in place for ophthalmology to operate more?"

"Yes, currently they are the flavor of the month, so to speak. The population is aging and cataracts need to be done. So they get the time. But it jibes with our numbers. They've been requesting more time for a few months now."

I'm sure Sam has, Mikaela thought sardonically. "I don't feel these past three months actually represent my department's long-term pattern," she pointed out. "There's the potential of another obstetrician joining. I've approached the hospital board about it and a financial audit is underway. If it goes through, we'll need one hundred percent of the OR time, and it will be filled. Right now, my practice is growing. The first three months don't reflect the actual need at all."

"Well, that may be so, but we have to look at what is happening now, not what might be needed three or six months from now."

"You said yourself that utilization is one hundred percent. Why can't it continue with the status quo for another six to twelve months until a more accurate pattern is established?" she asked.

"Well, it has been considered . . ." Dr. Crispin hesitated. "But there has been considerable pressure from ophthalmology."

"Have other solutions been considered?" Mikaela asked. "I wasn't even informed this was on the table and a decision being made." She reined in her temper. "I was given the position of department head so that the department would have a voice in this type of decision – one that could have serious impact on the future growth and recruitment of an obstetrician-gynecologist to Emerson. I don't think considerable pressure from ophthalmology is enough. I think the needs of the Department of Obstetrics and Gynecology should be heard as well."

"Well, there is a committee. It's made up of two members from the board of directors, myself as chief of surgery, the chief of staff, and four representatives from the various surgical specialties."

"Including ophthalmology?"

"Yes, one of the ophthalmologists is on the committee."

"I hope they're abstaining from voting."

"It hasn't really been put to a vote," Dr. Crispin said, leaning back in his chair. "I don't think anyone thought you'd mind. Your utilization is low and ophthalmology's is high. It seemed straightforward to balance things out."

"Well, actually, I do mind. I was given two days a week of OR time when I was recruited. It's not something I want to give away until I've had a chance to give it some careful consideration."

"That's certainly your privilege," Dr. Crispin said. "I hope you'll look at the bigger picture and as always, consider patient care as the number one priority." He opened a file and wrote a short note on a page. "The next meeting of the committee will be in one week. Perhaps you could let me know by then or put something in writing, so I can present it to the committee."

"Certainly," said Mikaela.

He closed the file and leaned forward, looking at her intently. "As you said, one of the pleasures, indeed one of the traditions, of working at Emerson is the teamwork and collegiality among the staff." He folded his hands into a triangle and tapped his chin thoughtfully. "Sometimes it involves compromise. Maybe it seems disappointing, even unfair, at the time. But then the tide turns and needs change, and that's taken into consideration. It's worked for us for many years, you understand, and we pride ourselves on its success. One could almost say it's the Emerson way." He looked over at her in silence.

Mikaela looked back without saying a word. Message sent and received, she thought bitterly.

He leaned back. "As I said, you've led the department well through many changes. It's a strength of your leadership." He stood.

Mikaela stood as well. "Thank you. I've enjoyed it. I'm learning that some change is necessary to move forward and grow. Would I be able to get a copy of that report?"

"Certainly. I'll have Gillian send you a copy first thing tomorrow."

"Thank you. And thank you for meeting with me and going over this. I'll look it over and put something in writing for you before next week."

Dr. Crispin nodded and came around to see her out.

"Good night," Mikaela said.

"Good night. Drive carefully. They were forecasting snow so the roads may be slippery."

Mikaela nodded and smiled and headed out. The smile quickly faded as she made her way back to her own office. She closed the door with a snap and sat down at her desk.

Chapter 26

Written in the Stars by Esmeralda Garnet
ARIES (March 21-April 19) The more information you gather, the more effective you will be. The situation is not what you expected it to be. Dig deeper.

That's the Emerson tradition, she mimicked sarcastically. Just lie down and let them walk all over you, she thought, crossing her arms across her chest and sitting back. That's the way it's always been done, she fumed. Just because it's always been done that way, doesn't mean it's the best way.

How can they look at a brand new practice pattern, one that's barely been established, and project that to the needs of the department for the future? Mikaela shook her head and picked up a pencil and started tapping the desk. She didn't want a title that didn't have any authority behind it to back it up. She was the department head and to her that meant she would have a voice in decision-making. She didn't want to be excluded and then be told what to do because everyone else got together and decided it was the best thing.

Where was the due process in that?

On top of that, Crispin implied she wouldn't be a team player, and wouldn't fit in at Emerson if she didn't agree. She'd be an outsider even before she had a chance to be an insider? Great. Just great. Mikaela threw the pencil on the desk. She could just go along with it, but what kind of precedent would be set doing that? How did she play this game?

And, what was behind this?

Not what. Who. Sam, Mikaela thought, that's who. He wants operating time and he wants it badly enough to put pressure on his department head and the committee. The squeaky wheel gets the grease. And of course, Sam fit right in with the old boys' club. So, what Sam wanted, he'd get. Wasn't that always the case? His job was more important than hers. It didn't matter that she was entitled to the operating time. That she had plans to build the department. It was about his needs being more important than hers. His job over her job. Again. God. It was Elliott all over. Mikaela stood up and paced in her office.

It didn't matter that her authority was undermined, that plans she put in place would be side railed, that it pitted her against other surgical departments. Until Sam got exactly what he wanted, he would continue to fight. He had the connections.

Mikaela huffed out a breath and ran her hand through her hair. They could be good in bed together, but if she looked for respect or equality out of bed, she wasn't going to find it. He went behind her back to get what he wanted. He didn't even have the courtesy to discuss it with her. Did he think so little of her? Did he see her position as a figurehead only?

Mikaela looked at the bobblehead, nodding thoughtlessly. Incensed, she swept it off the desk, into the garbage.

Mikaela wiped her eyes, ashamed for letting herself fall for another man of the same mold. Hadn't she learned anything from Elliott?

Well, Mikaela thought, it appears it's time for more change. Her chest squeezed at the thought and her resolve wavered and faltered for a fleeting moment. She sat down at her desk. As difficult as it was, deep down Mikaela knew she couldn't settle for this without looking for a better solution. She was hired for this job and took her role seriously, even if others didn't. So she'd look at the data and fight for what was best for her department. Diplomatically. Calmly. Assertively, in a politically correct way. But fight nonetheless. And she had a week to do it. So between clinics, operating, meetings, and deliveries, she would sort this out.

Her relationship with Sam was another whole issue. She needed to step back and take a hard look at what was happening there. Her heart broke just a little. Before she went any further, she needed to know what the hell was going on between them. It was too late to walk away without being hurt. But damned if she was going to put up with another man walking all over her and not respecting her for all of who she was.

I will not cry, I will not cry, she chanted. She rubbed the tears from her eyes. She had two more charts to finish and then she would go home. Home. His home, really. Mikaela sighed at how complicated change could be. Maybe she should start a list. Antagonize Department of Surgery. Confront Sam. Find new home. Boy, that all sounded like so much fun.

What she really needed was to call Margo and arrange for some Margo-time this weekend. Mikaela picked up her cell phone to send a text when her pager rang. Mikaela glanced at the number. Deliver babies, she mentally added to the list. Home and Sam would have to wait.

Chapter 27

happenstance horoscope

ARIES (March 21-April 19) Move forward and accept the inevitable. There are more possibilities open to you than you realize. Deal with what you've been given and don't back away.

The delivery had been complicated and Mikaela didn't finish until two o'clock in the morning. She debated, but in the end, too tired to care, decided to crash on her couch in her office. It didn't seem worth the effort to go home for the five hours she had before she was due back to start the clinic in the morning. Plus, although she knew she was being a coward and inventing excuses, she needed some distance from Sam.

It was late afternoon when Mikaela finally gathered her briefcase, signed off call and headed out. The plan was to drop by Sam's house, pack an overnight bag, and then drive to Rivermede, to her house. She had been texting Margo off and on throughout the day. They would meet at her house for dinner tonight. Tomorrow, they were going on a hike.

Margo belonged to the Trail-Heads Association, and they had organized a snowshoe hike for Saturday. Mikaela tried to slip out of it when she heard Margo's plans, but Margo wouldn't have it. The fresh air would clear her head, she didn't exercise enough, it was supposed to be a beautiful day, blah, blah, blah. Margo was worse than her mother. Both of their mothers. Knowing she was right didn't really help.

So they would indulge in take-out and a decadent dessert, maybe a movie with buttered popcorn tonight, and walk it off tomorrow. As much as she grumbled, Mikaela was really looking forward to spending time with Margo, even if it meant walking up a hill and back, for no good reason, for most of the day, in the snow. Who does that?

Mikaela had also sent a text off to Sam to let him know she'd be away for the weekend. They ping-ponged back and forth with texts, and she began to wonder if he sounded disappointed. She shook her head impatiently. When you started to analyze the *tone* of text messages, you really did need time away. And she would have time. And spend it hiking. Up and down a hill with no purpose. All day. In the cold. With a group of people who thought that was fun.

And that would be followed by more fun on Sunday. She would be spending tedious hours drafting a proposal explaining why she should keep her OR time instead of giving it to Sam – justifying keeping the hours she had been given a mere three months ago. Time that the board of directors deemed appropriate to a growing obstetrics department. The board of directors. Head honchos of the hospital. The ones who appointed her as department head.

Mikaela banged the steering wheel. She hated wasting her time, and justifying her department's OR time a mere three months after starting the job, was a waste of time. Except that if she didn't put the time in now, six months down the road when she needed two days a week, it would be gone. And Sam would have what he wanted at her expense. No, it wasn't going to happen, she resolved. She would enjoy tonight, endure tomorrow and on Sunday she would draft the best damn proposal the Department of Surgery had ever seen. And Sam could just go to hell. His mother was right. He was a dragon, an ox, and a goat.

Mikaela pulled into Sam's driveway and parked the car in front of the garage. Someone had widened the path in the snow to the front door, and the snow, which the sun had melted during the day, was freezing again into ice. She walked gingerly along. She wouldn't want to sprain her ankle and miss the big snowshoe hike.

The door opened silently as she pressed her finger to the pad. Her plan was to dash in and out again without speaking to Sam. Because right now she wasn't sure she could get through a conversation with him without screaming or shouting. Or worse, crying.

Mikaela blinked to wash away tears before they fell. She tried to hold onto anger, but it just hurt. She didn't want to believe he would do this to her. She loved him and thought, well hoped, wanted badly to believe, he loved her too. She so desperately wanted him to be okay with her job. He gave a good impression, damn him. He never said a negative word to her about her job. And all the while, behind the scenes this is what was playing out.

Mikaela felt betrayed. Like he had a mistress that she just discovered. And now she had to decide if she wanted to live with an ugly situation, pretend it didn't matter, keep work at work and home at home, or bring it all out into the open and let him know how much he hurt her. But to understand how much he hurt her, he would have to understand how much she cared, and she definitely wasn't ready to tell him. He didn't deserve her heart. The snake.

A wave of fatigue washed over her and her shoulders sagged under the weight of her briefcase. Mikaela slipped off her boots and leaving her coat on, walked silently to the bedroom. She collected what she needed for the weekend, and with her overnight case on one shoulder, picked up her briefcase and slipped on her boots.

Sam stood in the front hall watching her. Her head was down and her movements slow as she adjusted the weight of the bags and flicked her hair out from under the straps. She stopped abruptly when she saw him.

His smile faded when he saw the dark circles under her eyes, tears shimmering, and her unhappy expression. “Hey, what’s up?” he asked hesitantly.

“Nothing, just grabbing some stuff for the weekend,” she replied.

“I didn’t hear you come in.”

She shrugged and reached for her boots.

“Is everything okay?”

She stopped what she was doing and threw him a look, filled with disgust. She brushed away a tear impatiently.

The look had him stepping back, but the tears stopped him. He threw his hands in the air. “What?”

“I met with Bob Crispin yesterday.”

Sam watched her swallow and struggle to continue. He wanted to hold her and soothe her. He wanted to reach out and brush away the sadness. But she was holding herself stiffly, she wasn’t meeting his gaze, and inexplicably the anger seemed directed at him.

“He told me they’ve been tracking the use of my OR time.” She paused.

“Yeah. They do that with everyone.”

“Mmmhmm. Well, apparently, my first three months set the standard for my department. And the OR utilization committee,” she spat, “in its infinite wisdom and power, has decided to give away my time to a more deserving department.”

Sam said nothing. He shoved his hands in his pockets and considered what she said. Competition for OR time was so fierce, he could see it happening. Hell, even he had been bugging his department head for more time. Losing time would be a blow, especially for a new department. “Crispin seems like a straight shooter. Did you talk to him about this?”

"I tried. But apparently he's only one member on the committee. They thought I wouldn't mind." She shook her head in disgust. "I have a week to put together a proposal to justify why I should keep the time."

"Well, that's good. At least it's not a done deal."

"Yeah, right. I'm sure they've already made their decision. I can't honestly see how my presenting what they already know, or should know, will make a difference. They thought I wouldn't mind," she ranted. "How could you even think that, if you were a committee member? Not mind. Right. Obviously, they have another agenda entirely. Obviously, their priorities differ from mine."

"Make them see differently. You're the department head. You've developed a solid rep for negotiating change and making fair decisions even in the short time you've been here. I've heard nothing but positive comments about your work here."

Mikaela stood still and looked at him with wide eyes. She brushed away tears impatiently. "Really? So it wouldn't surprise you to hear that it's the department of ophthalmology putting all this pressure on? That they've demanded more time? That they've managed to put themselves on the committee and push all this through?"

Sam rocked back on his heels as it dawned on him why the anger was directed at him. "Aah," he said. "So you think I'm behind this?"

"Aren't you?" she snapped.

"You think I would go behind your back to get more OR time?"

"I think you did."

Sam felt anger flare and looked away. He nodded his head slowly and backed away, clearing a path for her to the door. "Well, I guess you have a week to sort it out," he acknowledged. "Have a good weekend."

“Thank you,” Mikaela said stiffly. “I’ll text you when I’m heading back.”

“Sure. Whatever.” Sam turned and headed to the kitchen.

Mikaela stared after him. Adjusting her bags, she wrenched open the front door and headed out to her car. She thought about slamming the door behind her, but she wouldn’t give him the satisfaction of showing him how much he hurt her.

Fine. Have a good weekend, she mimicked. Fine. Pig. Snake. Goat. We’ll see if you’ll get away with this. She slammed the car door shut and shoved the key in the ignition. Twisting it harder than she needed to, she started the engine.

I will not let another man interfere with my goals and ruin my job. I will not let another man make me unhappy. I will not fall in love with another man who does not respect me, and the work I do. She slumped in the seat and rested her forehead against the steering wheel.

Too late, she sniffled.

Chapter 28

Zodiac Zach – Don't leave home without him.

ARIES (March 21-April 19) Address partnerships and professional relationships head-on. It's important to keep your position clear if you want to avoid a misunderstanding. Being vague will lead to disappointment.

Sam listened to Mikaela leave. What the hell? Where the hell had that come from? He had no idea that his demands, no surely not, his *request*, for more OR time would have this impact. He just asked, for god's sake. How did it escalate into ruining what they had going? He had really been looking forward to this weekend. It was rare they both had it off, and he pictured them spending it together. They were good together, damn it. Outdoors, indoors, in the pool, in bed, he wanted to be with her.

So while he was figuring out how to make the engagement real, she was fingering him for pulling strings behind her back and screwing her. Nice. Great opinion she has of you, O'Brien. But why would she think that? Why would he do that?

Sure he'd jump at more OR time. It wasn't a secret. But why would she think he would do something underhanded to get it? Especially to her. Did she think so little of him? Sam rubbed his eyes, suddenly very tired. Of course, it wouldn't have anything to do with the fact that he was asking her to live a lie. That her whole world was turned upside down by the fallout. But she had done so well. She had the sweetest set-up. Why was it such a big deal?

Because it was all lies and deceit. Their whole relationship was based on lies and deceit. And how could she trust a liar? Why would he think she would?

This relationship crap was bullshit. He knew he wasn't any good at it. He couldn't even make a fake engagement work. What a joke. It was too much work and even if he was willing to stick his neck out, she wouldn't trust him. He would always be the liar and cheat making her life miserable. She'd be questioning his motives and believing the worst before he was even aware they had a problem. And when they have a problem, she just up and leaves? Whatever happened to sticking around, talking about it, working it out?

Sam winced as he listened to himself. Jeez, how many times had he heard that and dismissed it as he walked out the door and moved on? One night stand, one week, one month, it didn't matter. He couldn't be bothered. It was never worth the effort or the time to get into a discussion. If there was a problem, he would move on. End of problem.

His gut clenched as he stared outside into the darkness. She'd come back. She would take some time to cool off and she'd come back. They would sit down and have a *discussion*. Even if it killed him.

He would tell her how he felt. Sweat broke out on his brow and his heart raced. He rocked back on his heels. Maybe not. Maybe he would just start with an explanation about the OR time. Ease into this discussion thing. Plain and simple. Find out what was going on in her head and fix it. Sam winced. No, um, find out what she thought he had done and clear it up.

He frowned.

The trouble was he did want more OR time. Looks like he had a weekend to figure out how badly.

Chapter 29

Written in the Stars by Esmeralda Garnet

ARIES (March 21-April 19) How you treat others will be influenced by how others treat you. Listen to both sides of the story before you take action.

Later that night, Mikaela invited Margo in and pulled her close for a fierce hug.

"Hey," Margo said as she stepped back, noting the strained look on Mikaela's face. Mikaela was wearing sweatpants and a sweatshirt. Comfort clothes, Margo thought.

"Come in," Mikaela said. "I ordered Indian food and it just arrived so we should eat it while it's hot."

"Sounds good. I haven't had Indian for a while," Margo said. She took off her coat and threw it on the nearby banister and followed Mikaela into the kitchen.

Mikaela pulled out the dishes and set the kitchen table.

"I picked up a caramel pear cheesecake for dessert. There's a new bakery downtown and I was tempted by the chocolate creations, but the caramel had my name on it," Margo said as she set the box on the counter.

Mikaela laughed, and Margo breathed a sigh of relief as she watched her friend relax just a little.

Margo grabbed the cutlery for the table.

"Wine?" Mikaela asked, holding up a red and a white.

"Absolutely."

Mikaela picked a pinot gris, twisted off the cap, and filled two glasses. She handed one to Margo as she sipped her own and gestured for them to sit down.

"I ordered chicken korma, shrimp jalfreezi, saag paneer, cauliflower bhaji, and palao rice. And naan. So help yourself," Mikaela invited.

They filled their plates with a little of everything and ripped a naan bread in half to share.

"The shrimp dish is spicy," Margo commented as she scooped another mouthful. "I like it."

"It is good. I like the korma, too."

"Something about food I don't have to cook just feeds my soul," Margo said.

"Amen to that." Mikaela smiled. "So catch me up on things. How's work?"

"Work is good. My practice is as busy as I want it to be, and the painting is surprisingly busy for this time of year," Margo admitted. "You know how they're redoing the Lakeview Suites? And I was really bummed because Chloe and I put in a bid for the contract and we didn't get it?"

Mikaela nodded. "Yes, I've boycotted them since."

Margo laughed. "Well, you can stay there again. It turns out, the company that won the bid underestimated the job. No surprise there, for me, anyway." She grinned. "They have a completion clause, and they've realized they're not going to finish on time. So they subcontracted the work to us, and there's enough work to take us into January, I figure.

"Plus, one the busiest times for the hotel is over Christmas, and they've asked us to take a break from December twenty-second until the twenty-seventh. Which is great. So Chloe and I will have steady work into the New Year, and we'll get a break over Christmas. We're not the primary contact, so we don't have to waste time sorting out paint colors, coordinating with designers, or dealing with the paperwork. In short, the administrative shit. We just show up, paint, and go home. It couldn't have worked out any better," she beamed.

"That's perfect."

"I know. I'm very happy. Last year it was difficult getting jobs through the winter. This year definitely looks better. And," she said, waving her fork, "Bennett Homes should be ready for painting starting in February. They started to build a new subdivision in the fall, and they should be finished at the end of January or beginning of February. And we did win the contract for that one," she said, winking, "so we'll be set into the spring when homeowners start thinking about renovations. It'll work perfectly."

"Your connection with Trace Bennett have anything to do with winning that contract?" she asked, raising her eyebrows and smiling.

"Most definitely did," Margo said with a huge grin.

"They're lucky to have you do the job," Mikaela said.

"Well, I don't know about that . . . "

"No really. You show up on time, start when you say you will. Your work is exceptional, you finish when you promise, and you clean up the site afterward. Not all painters are as reliable or as talented," Mikaela said in earnest.

"Well, thank you," Margo said with a laugh. "If I ever need a reference, I'll get them to call you."

"My pleasure."

"And how are things with your job?" Margo asked. She was disappointed to see the smile disappear and the tension show in Mikaela's face the minute the words were out.

"It's fine. There's a bit of a tug of war going on for operating room time, which is creating some friction."

"Ah, administrative shit."

"Exactly. The medicine is great. The administrative shit, as you so succinctly put it, is a headache."

Margo paused. "Why is it making you sad?"

Mikaela looked surprised.

"Dark circles, tears. Something's bothering you."

"You know, you could just be polite and not mention my haggard appearance."

"Well I could, but then I wouldn't be the best friend I obviously am."

Mikaela just harrumphed.

"You know, since you started this job, I've seen you handle tons of administrative shit. At first I worried about the workload for you. But whenever you talked about it, you had this energy about you. Your eyes were shining, you talked about it excitedly, like you were enjoying the challenge. But this is the first time I've seen you . . . sad. It's like the balloon popped and you're the deflated version of it."

Mikaela grimaced. She toyed with the napkin ring. "I guess because this time it involves Sam."

"Sam? How?"

"Sam wants more OR time. And he's probably going to get it, too. But he's taking it from my department and he's doing it through the chief of surgery."

"Sam is? Why would he do that?"

"Because he really wants it. And because he figures he can. After all, it comes down to his job or mine. And of course, his is more important." She shook her head in disgust.

"Jeez. Shades of Elliott all over again," Margo murmured.

"Exactly," Mikaela exclaimed, leaning back in her chair.

"What did he say when you talked to him about it?"

"He said 'have a good weekend.'"

"What?"

"Yeah. I told him that I was coming here and would have to spend the weekend writing a proposal to justify keeping my OR time, and he said to have a good weekend."

Margo was silent. That sounded like the beginning of the end. "That's it? Was it like 'have a good weekend' with a smile and wave, or was it 'have a good weekend' I'm so guilty I can't look you in the eye?"

Mikaela frowned. "More like 'have a good weekend' I don't care, I'm walking away."

Margo grimaced. Ouch. "And no explanation about why he went behind your back to organize this?"

"Nope."

"Did he talk to you about it before? I mean, did you know he was going to do this?"

"Nope. The chief of surgery asked to meet with me and informed me that because I haven't used all my time, they were taking it and giving it to ophthalmology, who have been requesting more."

"I find this hard to believe. Sam really seems into you. I can't believe he would do something so underhanded."

"Yeah, it's not like he ever lies or anything."

"Mmmm. You do have a point there. But really, maybe he just requested extra time and didn't have control over the rest. You know how these things can spiral out of control."

"Yeah. That I do know. But he's so aggressive with it."

"What happens if he doesn't get more OR time?"

"I don't know. I haven't really discussed it with him. His skills get rusty maybe? His waiting list gets too long? One of the reasons he left the General was because they were going to cut his OR time."

"So it's important enough for him to be aggressive. He wants it so he puts a bug in his department's head, haha excuse the pun, who runs with it and gets the chief of surgery on his side. Sam may have been left out of the loop beyond talking to his head. I don't know. I'm speculating. But it might be worth sitting down and talking it out further. If it matters to you."

Mikaela sighed. "Yeah, unfortunately it does."

"I guess you just have to decide what matters more."

"What do you mean?"

"I don't know. Maybe I don't know enough about the whole thing. But it sounds like you could be pulling an Elliott on Sam."

"What? How?"

"Well. Sam versus OR time. Sam needs more OR time and you have a chance to help him out. You feel your department is more important so you don't, but by putting your job ahead of him, you jeopardize his job and your relationship with him. You Elliott him." She shrugged.

Mikaela just stared. "What?" Tears filled her eyes.

Margo panicked. "Sorry. No. Not really. It's completely different. Just pretend I didn't say that. How about some dessert? That pear cheesecake looks delicious." She stood up and collected their plates.

Mikaela didn't move. "Am I? Elliotting him?"

With a sigh, Margo set the dishes on the counter and sat down and covered Mikaela's hand with her own. "Talk to him, Mikaela. Find out what Sam thinks. Maybe there's a solution you both can live with. If you care enough, let him know."

"You make it sound so easy," Mikaela complained.

Margo wiped a tear from Mikaela's cheek. "I know. Giving advice is always easier than following it. Especially when I have no idea what I'm talking about." She smiled. "Feel free to tell me to mind my own business and stick with painting. I'm good at painting."

"You are good at painting. And for being there when I need you. And for saying things I need to hear. Even when I don't want to hear them. I love you, you know."

"I love you, too." Margo gave Mikaela's hand a quick squeeze. "And just remember that. Tomorrow when your feet are complaining, and your nose is cold, you love me."

"Maybe not that much."

"Too late. One o'clock start. How about some cheesecake?"

"Sounds good. I feel the need to carbo load."

Margo laughed. "I'll give you a big piece."

Chapter 30

Written in the Stars by Esmeralda Garnet

ARIES (March 21-April 19) Take care of work-related matters. Being practical and looking out for yourself should be your first priority. Don't allow a partnership to come between you and your common sense. Don't hesitate when change is required.

Mikaela sat sipping her coffee the next morning while she scanned the newspaper and read her horoscope. Put herself first. She rubbed her tired eyes. If she'd read that yesterday, she might not have been awake half the night worrying about what to do.

She needed to talk to Sam. Margo was right about that. Maybe she had been too hasty in questioning his motives and assuming the worst. She needed to talk to him, find out how it all happened and what it all meant to him.

But what troubled her more was Margo's suggestion that she might be Elliotting Sam. Mikaela cringed. She hadn't meant to. She was trying to find a balance between asserting her role as department head and fitting in with the rest of the hospital, keeping her options open for the future while trying to please the Department of Surgery, and dealing with how she felt about Sam while living a lie in a fake engagement. She didn't want to lie anymore, or be lied to anymore. And she definitely didn't want to use her job to hurt Sam.

Expanding the department and hiring another obstetrician were important goals. There was too much work for one doctor, and she didn't want to be on call for high-risk deliveries twenty-four seven. She needed to share call or she would burn out. And then nobody would be happy, least of all her.

She could give the time to Sam. It could take six months or more to complete the hiring process, and in the meantime, Sam could operate. It was frustrating, though. She might never get the time back, or it would be an argument when she needed it. Sam wouldn't be in the midst of it, but she would.

She got up and carried her coffee cup to the sink to rinse it.

She had two hours to look over all the information from Crispin, before she had to meet Margo and the gang for snowshoeing. Maybe a brilliant idea would come to her.

She took the file out of her briefcase, grabbed the mail piled on the counter, and sat down at her desk. She threw the flyers into the recycling bin and placed the bills in a pile. An envelope from Winmarket Regional Hospital made her pause.

A while back, she had sent a letter to Winmarket Regional. It was a smaller hospital with a decent-sized obstetrics department in a growing community. At the time, that's what she wanted. She hadn't heard back and had assumed the position had been filled.

Mikaela ripped open the letter.

Dear Dr. Finn,

We have reviewed your application for full-time associate staff in the Department of Obstetrics and Gynecology at Winmarket Regional Hospital. We would like to invite you for an interview. The position is effective July 1.

Winmarket Regional Hospital is situated in the middle of a vibrant community offering a diversity of cultural, recreational, and educational opportunities. We are proud of the excellence in healthcare provided to the growing community and catchment area of 200,000+.

Please contact us by January 7 to arrange an interview. We look forward to meeting with you.

Sincerely,
P. Reginald BA MSc MD FRCPS

She blew her hair out of her eyes. That was exactly what she needed. Six months ago. It would have been so easy. Compared to what she was dealing with now, the position at Winmarket was perfect.

Maybe this was the answer. Maybe this was the change she should make. Maybe this was the change that was meant to be. It wasn't too late. She could start fresh and start honestly.

What about Sam?

They could 'break up' by July. They could tell people it didn't work out. Sam could stay at Emerson and live in his house, and she could be far away where it wouldn't hurt to see him every day. And she wouldn't be caught in the middle of a problem that had the potential to hurt them both. Her heart would heal. Probably. Hopefully.

Her chest ached just thinking about it. Butterflies in her stomach churned and she felt lightheaded. It was a big scary change that wouldn't include Sam. It would be exciting and healthy, Mikaela told herself sternly.

Why did it make her want to cry?

Mikaela glanced at the clock and realized she needed to get ready if she was going to meet Margo on time. The file sat unopened. She fleetingly thought of texting Margo to bow out, but Margo would just come and drag her along. Maybe the fresh air would clear her head and give her a fresh perspective. Either way, it couldn't hurt.

Chapter 31

happenstance horoscope

ARIES (March 21-April 19) A change of direction may be beneficial. New challenges are part of emotional and physical growth. Don't dwell on the past.

Oh, she was wrong about that. Muscles in her calves and thighs complained bitterly. Mikaela hoped she could walk tomorrow.

The temperature was perfect for a walk. Clean, fresh snow covered the ground, and the treetops glistened an iridescent white in the sunshine. They were walking up a steady incline on a path among evergreen trees.

She expected the snowshoes to look like wooden tennis rackets and was surprised to be handed sleek lightweight aluminum frames. She felt light as a feather walking over the deep snow banks.

But oh, someone might have mentioned what a workout it was. She sweat through the first two layers she wore and hoped there was a little Palent technology magic working in the fabric. She was definitely going to feel it tomorrow. But the good news – she was distracted enough not to worry about the problems at work. For that alone, she was glad she came.

For all her effort, the group kept a leisurely pace and stopped after an hour and a half for a snack of nuts and dried fruit. They sipped bottles of water. Some stood, some sat on rocks cleared of snow, enjoying the quiet and the warm stream of sunshine through the canopy. No crickets, no frogs, no snapping twigs this time of year. Even the birds were quiet. A chickadee fluttered silently down and landed briefly on an outstretched hand holding seeds, and just as quietly darted off again to the trees, leaving a smile of pleasure on the bird feeder.

Margo sauntered over to Mikaela and smiled. "How are you doing?"

"I'm great. It's a bit more than the 'walk in the park' you promised," she said with a laugh. "But I'm loving it. This is a little oasis in the forest."

"I know. It's great company for the mind, exercise for the body, and this serene spot for the spirit."

Laughter spilled over from a group as they put their snowshoes back on. "They seem like a really great bunch," Mikaela said as she watched them.

"They are. Some of them have hiked all over the world and have stories that would curl your hair. And that's just the teenagers."

"I can't keep up with the lead. And he looks like he's my dad's age."

"Seventy-two. His wife is just as fit. She didn't come today because their granddaughter had a baby, and she's gone to visit. But the two of them are still active in the triathlon circuit. They do it for fun, they say. For fun." Margo shook her head.

Mikaela laughed as she stood up, slipped her boot into the snowshoe and tightened it. "That's what I keep telling myself. This is fun. This is fun." She grinned over at Margo. "But I wouldn't want to overdo it with the fun. You know, too much of a good thing and all that, so we are, ah, heading back soon, right?"

Margo laughed. "Yes. The path is a big loop, and this is about the halfway point."

"Good. At the end of the day, when I'm home and feeling good about spending the day outside in the fresh air, proud of myself for pushing myself that extra mile . . . there's caramel cheesecake waiting for me in my fridge."

"More fun. Enough to share?"

"Of course. Is there any other way to eat cheesecake?"

"You're a bad influence," Margo pointed out as she tightened her second snowshoe. She gestured for Mikaela to go ahead and moved to join the group.

"You bought the cheesecake," Mikaela said as she fell in line.

"I was just doing my part to prevent world hunger."

"One small slice at a time. That's beautiful."

"Thank you."

"And I shall reward you with cheesecake. There's leftover Indian, too."

"Thank you. I will humbly accept."

Later that night as Mikaela savored the last of the cheesecake from her plate, she blurted, "I got a letter from Winmarket Regional Hospital about a job offer."

"What?" Margo stopped with her fork halfway to her mouth.

"Winmarket is looking for an ob-gyn. I applied a while ago and had forgotten about it, but I got a letter in the mail inviting me for an interview."

"Really?"

Mikaela nodded. "I opened it this morning. The job would start the first of July."

Margo sat back in her chair. "What about Emerson?" What about Sam? she thought, but didn't say it out loud.

"I would give them notice, and since I've already started the process to hire someone, they'll have an obstetrician."

Mikaela leaned forward. "I just think it would be best. I can't go on with this fake engagement forever. We said a year and July first will almost be a year. Sam's established and can carry on. After we end the engagement, I can't stay and risk seeing him every day. I just couldn't do it. And I don't think I'm cut out to be the department head. Look what's happening. If I do what's best for the department, I hurt Sam. If I do what's best for Sam, I hurt the department. I can't do this. At least, not at the same hospital as Sam. I could start fresh without the lies."

"Wow. That's a big change. Is it really what you want?"

"What I really want doesn't seem possible."

Margo handed Mikaela a tissue and reached over and gave her hand a squeeze. "Hey, don't cry."

"Sorry," Mikaela apologized. She wiped her eyes and straightened her shoulders. "Yes, this is what I want. You know me. Big scary change is what I crave," she smiled through watery eyes.

Margo chuckled quietly. "Yup, you to a tee," she smiled sympathetically.

"Winmarket is only about an hour away from here so we'd still see each other."

"I'm counting on it," Margo agreed. "When do you have to let them know?"

"Early January, so I have a couple of weeks."

Margo nodded silently. A lot could happen in a couple of weeks. "And Christmas in the meantime. Do you have time off?"

"I'm working the twenty-fourth then taking off between the twenty-fifth and the twenty-ninth."

"Nice. Are you visiting your folks?"

"Yes, I'll head there for dinner on the twenty-fifth for a couple of days. I'll see how it goes. Maybe longer."

"They'll like that," Margo said.

"Yeah. You're welcome to come, you know. They always love to see you."

"Thanks, I know. Trace has time off and we'll spend time with his family and my mom. I hope to have some time alone with him, too." She wiggled her eyebrows.

Mikaela smiled. "Hiking? Snowshoeing?"

"Of course. I'm all about the physical activity."

"Well, I thoroughly enjoyed the après-snowshoeing activity," Mikaela agreed.

"It was a good day. Tomorrow I'm back at work. Are you staying here or heading back to Emerson?"

"I'll probably go back tomorrow afternoon."

Margo nodded and covered a yawn. "Well, I should head home and get some sleep. I'm glad you came today."

"Me, too. Thanks for dragging me along."

Mikaela stood and followed Margo to the front door. Margo slipped her coat on and Mikaela caught her in a close hug.

"Keep me posted," Margo said.

"I will."

"And talk to Sam."

Mikaela sighed. "I will."

Chapter 32

Zodiac Zach – Don't leave home without him.

ARIES (March 21-April 19) Persevere and the challenge will be within your reach. Dialogue is important but actions speak louder than words. Do your own thing to ensure your happiness and satisfaction.

The next morning Mikaela sat at her kitchen table with a steaming cup of coffee at her elbow, flipping through the operating room files and making notes on her computer. She took another sip of coffee and tried to see this from Sam's perspective.

If you just looked at the statistics, laid out in black and white, the allotment of time did look unfair. However, there was no mention of hers being a new department or one with the potential to grow in the next year. Nor were there any remarks about her utilization being one hundred percent. She noted that the Ear, Nose and Throat specialists gave up operating time and worse, released it too late to be used. She played with the numbers, considered the options, and wondered if there was a compromise that would work. Mikaela tapped a pencil rhythmically on the table and chewed her lip as she studied it. Finally, she shoved her pencil absentmindedly behind her ear and hunched over her computer.

If she gave up 2.3 units and the ENT specialists gave up 1.7, which was their average underutilization, ophthalmology could gain a full day. That would still leave 5.7 for her department, which she felt she could use now and share later with a new obstetrician. If she left in July, it was plenty of operating time for the new obstetrician, with enough wiggle room if they wanted to entice a partner to the hospital. It seemed fair. Mikaela tried to look at it objectively. ENT would have to agree to the plan, but looking at the numbers, it wouldn't change the essence of what they were using now. Maybe the numbers alone didn't tell the whole story, but she hoped it would work.

She typed it up, explained her reasoning, included the statistics, and fancied up the language. Content that she had created a strong argument for a compromise, she saved it and shut down her computer.

Mikaela stood and stretched, rolled her neck, and grimaced at the stiffness in her thigh and calf muscles.

She wanted a swim.

She needed to talk with Sam. Butterflies churned in her stomach. Nerves? Hunger? Mikaela wasn't sure, but it was one o'clock, and she hadn't eaten lunch, so she could start with that.

She ate a quick sandwich and tidied the condo, ready to leave. She packed her overnight case and briefcase and locked the door behind her.

It was a cloudy day, but the roads were clear for her drive back. Sunday drivers slowed traffic on one stretch of highway through the country. A car in front of her had customized license plates that read RYLFLUSH. Royal Flush, she thought. What's the story behind that? Did they own a bath store specializing in toilets? Buy their car from poker money? Menopausal hot flashes? Maybe it was better not to know, she chuckled.

Mikaela pulled up beside Sam's car in the driveway, her hope that he wasn't going to be home just yet, dashed. Gathering her belongings, she went to the front door and let herself in.

Sam heard the front door close. She came back. A wave of relief coursed through him. Don't blow it this time, he told himself sternly.

He stood back and studied the Scotch pine tree that towered above him. It hadn't seemed that tall when he cut it down the day before. He bent down and adjusted the stand.

"Oh, that looks lovely! What a great tree! And the smell of fresh pine is wonderful," Mikaela said as she walked into the room.

Sam looked over and smiled. "Thanks. My mom sent some Christmas decorations, so I thought I'd better get a tree. I wasn't sure if you'd want to help choose it, but I figured we could decorate it together."

Mikaela flushed with pleasure. "I'd love to help. Did you get any lights?"

Sam nodded at a bag on the sofa. "In there. I'm just about done if you want to open them."

Mikaela pulled out three packages of multicolored lights.

"I hope you're not a white light kinda person."

"Not at all." Mikaela ripped open the packaging and unwound the string of lights. She plugged them in to check they worked and laid them out over the sofa ready to go on the tree.

Sam wandered into the kitchen and pressed a remote. The cheerful notes of a Christmas song filled the room. "Would you like a drink? Wine or eggnog?" he asked from the kitchen.

"Eggnog, please," Mikaela answered.

Sam walked over and handed her a glass. "Cheers," he said as he clinked his glass against hers.

"Cheers." Mikaela smiled and sipped her drink. "Mmmm . . . delicious," she said. "I can taste the rum."

Sam eyed the lights. "Think there'll be enough? I wasn't sure how many we'd need."

"Two hundred lights per string. Looks like a lot." She grinned. She set down her glass and picked up the first string, weaving them into the depth of the tree in different layers. Sam followed, handing her the lights and keeping them from getting tangled. When the last of the string was nestled in the branches, they plugged it in and stood back to admire it.

"There are a lot of lights," Mikaela said.

Sam laughed. "It looks great though."

"I love it. Where are the decorations?"

Sam handed her a box, brushing his hand against hers. Mikaela lifted the lid and looked inside. The box was filled with crystal stars, little beaded elves, and glass Santas holding an array of colorful presents. And of course, a little Aries ram with a Santa hat and a scorpion with lights.

"These are adorable." She carefully lifted each one out, fastened a hook, and handed them to Sam to hang.

When the box was empty, Sam picked up his drink and sat down on the sofa and eyed the tree. "Needs tinsel," he observed.

Mikaela sat beside him on the sofa and groaned. "No. No tinsel. It'll ruin it."

"What? You gotta have tinsel. It makes it all sparkly."

"There are six hundred lights. There's plenty of sparkle."

"Obviously you're an amateur tree decorator. All the pros add tinsel."

Mikaela laughed. "I haven't decorated a tree in years. I was either working or visiting my parents, and their tree was always decorated by the time I arrived. I love it." She sipped her eggnog. "Speaking of my parents, my mom was asking if we could visit over the holiday."

"Sure, it shouldn't be a problem." Sam kept his tone even and worked at being nonchalant. Mikaela hadn't mentioned introducing him to her parents in all the time they'd been together. Normally a 'meet my parents' request was his sign to dodge. He couldn't run fast enough or far enough away. But with a tug of anxiety, he realized this time was different. He wanted a life together and a real engagement. He had no idea what she wanted, but meeting her parents was a step in the right direction. "I have the week around Christmas off."

"Maybe we could go there for dinner on Christmas day and stay for a couple of days?"

Sam nodded. "That would work." He sipped his eggnog. They needed to talk about Friday. He didn't like it, didn't want to rock the boat, but it had to be said. Just rip the Band-Aid off, he told himself. "Look, about Friday . . . I didn't mean to cause a problem with your job when I requested more OR time. Or with us. If I don't make any noise, nothing ever changes. I thought I needed to start making waves early, but I certainly didn't expect it to create the ripple effect it did. I'm really sorry it affected you."

Mikaela looked down at her hands. "I'm sorry that I reacted the way I did on Friday. I was frustrated and tired, but I shouldn't have blamed you."

"Why did you?"

Mikaela sighed. "They told me ophthalmology was taking my time. I knew you were asking for more, so I figured you were using your connection with me to get it."

"And that made you mad?"

Mikaela tried to explain. "I was more sad than mad. Sad that you didn't talk to me about it. Sad that my position was being undermined. Sad that the committee didn't even involve me in the discussion."

"I didn't know it would involve you."

"I know. I know that now. I'm sorry."

"I've heard nothing but positive things about the job you're doing. I don't think anyone would question your commitment or your authority."

"Thanks." Mikaela looked at him. "But frankly, I don't know if I'm cut out for this job. I like the clinical work," she said quickly. "But the administrative stuff . . ." She shrugged.

"Really? I think you're great at it. It takes a lot of patience and skill to make everyone feel like they're heard and their opinions matter. And you've done that. You've weathered a lot of change in the past three months. I've heard you listen to nursing staff, patients, admin, everyone, and come up with creative solutions that work. It's a gift."

Tears welled in Mikaela's eyes. Sam smiled gently and pulled Mikaela close.

Mikaela closed her eyes and then moved restlessly. "Winmarket is looking for an obstetrician, and they've invited me for an interview."

"Winmarket?"

She nodded. "I applied when I finished my residency and forgot about it. But a few days ago, I received a letter from them."

"You've got a job here."

"I know. But this would be a clinical position. I wouldn't have to be the department head."

"Really? And you'd want that?" he asked. "Are there any openings for ophthalmology?"

"Ophthalmology? I don't know. Why?"

"For me."

"For you?"

She sounded so surprised. Sam paused. "This is just for you," he said finally.

"Well, I thought it would give us a fresh start. You could stay here. We wouldn't have to pretend we're engaged and live in a pack of lies."

Sam pulled his arm away. "I see. So you would just leave."

"Well, the position starts in July. By then we were going to break up anyway, right?"

"Right," Sam said slowly.

"This way I could leave, and you could stay. Live here. You'll be settled into the hospital."

"Right."

"I could start a new job in a new hospital without all this deception."

Sam was silent. "Sounds like you've thought this through."

"Some. I spent this weekend writing the proposal to adjust the OR time. I realized I'm not cut out for this. I can't be cutthroat and aggressive and demanding. It's just not me. But I can't sit back and do nothing." She sighed. "It takes too much energy trying to fit in between."

"Maybe that's the point," Sam said quietly. "Maybe you should just be yourself. You don't have to be aggressive, but you don't have to be passive either. Just be you. Seems to have worked pretty well for the past three months."

"I haven't had any major problems to deal with though."

Sam shrugged. "Designing and implementing a new suite, working with hospital administrators, contractors and architects all while keeping the nursing staff, patients and other docs happy. Seems like a tall order to me." Sam glanced at Mikaela's unhappy face. He leaned his head back. "But what the hell do I know? I left the General because I couldn't stand all the extra administrative crap." He took a swig of his drink. "You should do what makes you happy." Disappointment coursed through Sam as Mikaela sat silently. "Well, sounds like that's the plan. We continue this charade for another six months, then you bail," he said, trying to keep the anger and frustration out of his voice.

Mikaela started to argue, but stopped.

"Fine. I'm going for a swim." Sam got up, banged his empty glass down on the counter in the kitchen, and strode out of the room.

Sam cut threw the water angrily. That went well, he thought sarcastically. Great *discussion.* He couldn't believe that while he plotted to make the engagement real, she was plotting out how to end it and move away. Great. Now he knew how she felt. What a fiasco. At least he kept his mouth shut and didn't make a fool of himself. Sam cut through the water, flipped at the wall, and pushed off with a powerful kick. He didn't want her to take another job. He didn't want her to move out. He wanted her to love him like he loved her. Pain seared his chest. He pounded the water until his arms ached and his breath caught. So now what? He has to pretend he's fine with the whole stupid plan? Every day, he has to sit with her and be happy for her? Live out this fake engagement knowing that in the end, she's leaving? It was going to be a long six months.

Mikaela sat quietly, blinking away tears. Guilt clawed at her. She could have made him happy, she felt like screaming. She had the chance to make his life easier, to make his job better, but did she? No, she put her job first. What did that say about her? About them? It's for the best, she told herself as her eyes filled. She focused on the Christmas tree, the pretty lights, and the sparkle of the ornaments. She wanted to curl up beside Sam and start Christmas traditions together. Staring at the tree just made her sadder. Mikaela got up restlessly. She picked up her bag in the front hall. As she walked through the kitchen and past the exercise room, she saw Sam swimming lengths in the pool. She watched him cut gracefully through the water with powerful strokes, his skin gleaming in the low lights. Oh Sam, she thought, I'm so sorry. She turned away and made her way down the hall. She hesitated outside the guest room. Guest room? Master bedroom? She walked into the guest room and dumped her bags on the floor. It was going to be a long six months.

Chapter 33

happenstance horoscope

ARIES (March 21-April 19) Your ideas are solid — now all you have to do is make them work. It's best to be honest to put an end to a difficult situation. Consider another person's viewpoint. Love is yours.

By Thursday, Mikaela's nerves were wrung so tight she was surprised her hair wasn't curling spontaneously. She had dropped off the proposal on Monday and hadn't yet heard back from the committee. She had operated all day Tuesday and had a fully booked clinic on Wednesday. She'd slept fitfully all week and missed the easy camaraderie she had had with Sam. He worked, swam, slept, and avoided her like the plague. Maybe he'd had a chance to think about how she treated him and decided she was as unlikable as she felt.

And worst of all, the Department of Surgery's Christmas dinner and dance started in one hour. She dreaded it. They had hardly spoken to each other since Sunday, and tonight they would have to pretend they were a happily engaged couple.

Mikaela dragged herself into the shower and let the warm water soothe her tired muscles. She stood under the stream and wished her problems could be washed away. If only she could rewind the clock and start with the truth. The whole truth. It would be so simple. She could tell Sam she loved him. He would tell her . . . well, she wasn't really sure what he would tell her. Mikaela sighed. She wanted to hear that she was the love of his life, and he couldn't live without her. That he wanted to marry her and spend a lifetime of Christmases with her. And their children. Cute little Sams and Mikaelas.

She turned off the shower and wrapped herself in a fluffy towel. She rubbed her hair dry and combed it out. Or at least, she wished, they could go back to being friends. Eating together, spending the evenings together. She missed that. Since Sunday, they had barely seen each other. Sam suddenly got extremely busy.

Mikaela pulled the red velvet dress over her head and smoothed it over her hips. The material clung to her curves and draped softly to her thighs. She fastened a single teardrop necklace and pulled her hair up, leaving soft tendrils to hide the jewels that sparkled at her ears. She fussed with her make-up and took extra care to hide the dark circles under her eyes. Dabbing her favorite perfume behind her ears, she slipped into her heels and headed out to the living room.

They planned to drive together. Thankfully it wasn't far because her nerves were already screaming and the butterflies in her stomach in overdrive.

Sam looked gorgeous. If the whole tall, dark, and handsome thing he had going didn't make her heart stumble, then the addition of the brooding, sexy expression did. Worse, she knew what was under that perfectly tailored suit.

Mikaela plastered a fake smile on her face and stepped into the room. Sam looked up, and she faltered at the hunger that flashed in his eyes. He dropped his gaze and when he glanced at her again, it was with the disdain that had plagued her in the past week.

"Ready to go?"

"I am."

He helped her with her coat, being careful not to touch her, and held the car door open. The ride to the banquet hall was thankfully short. There was only so much you could say about the weather without the air becoming tense and awkward.

Once they entered the hall, Sam held her hand and smiled naturally. He greeted others and introduced Mikaela warmly to those she hadn't met. They sat beside each other at dinner and, despite the enormous effort it took to appear like a happy couple, they laughed and joked with the others at the table.

The tables were cleared and the music started. They continued to socialize with the couples around them until the others got up to dance, and they were the only ones left sitting at the table.

"Would you like to dance?" Sam asked.

Mikaela glanced over, but she couldn't read his expression. "Sure."

Sam stood and held out his hand to help her up. She could feel the pressure of his hand in the small of her back as he followed her to the dance floor.

Mikaela turned and held her arms out stiffly for the embrace, but he pulled her close and held her against him. She rested her arm across his shoulders and his soft hair brushed her hand. With her leg between his, she felt the ripple of his thigh as he glided her around the floor. Mikaela was caught up in the sensation of his body against hers and shivered without hearing what he whispered in her ear.

He pulled back slightly and smiling for the first time in a week, repeated what he said. "I hear I have you to thank for the extra OR time."

She struggled to focus.

"Your proposal went through and I've been given an extra day of OR time."

"Really? That's great. I didn't realize they'd made a decision."

"Thank you."

Guilt swamped her. "Please don't thank me."

"Why?" He drew back in surprise. "You gave up a chunk of time and because of your ideas, I gained a full day."

"Well, I'm glad. Really I am. But my first instinct was to protect the department, and I'm not very proud of that," she admitted.

"Why not? That's what you're supposed to do. That's why you're the department head."

"But it was you. I knew it was you who needed the time."

"Fair enough. But the responsibility didn't, and shouldn't, rest solely with you. Your responsibility should be to patient care and your department. That just makes sense."

"Really? It doesn't upset you that I didn't put you first?"

"Of course not. Not for this. Now, if you considered a new job and picked a hospital that didn't need an ophthalmologist, that, *that* might upset me."

She stared at him. "That upset you?" she asked, unsure whether he was joking or not.

He didn't answer as the music transitioned into another slow song.

"Sam? Did that upset you?"

"Yes, that did."

"Why?"

Sam debated. He couldn't go on like he had this past week. Living with her, but not living with her had killed him. Not living with her at all he couldn't fathom. "I don't want you to take another job and live in another city. Unless I'm with you."

"You don't?"

"No, I don't."

He pulled back and looked into her eyes. "I love you, Mikaela. I want to be with you wherever you are. I can leave the house and the job. I can't live without you."

"Really?" Mikaela beamed.

"Really."

Mikaela hugged him close. "I love you. I didn't want to leave you, but I couldn't stay and watch you with someone else after the year was up."

"I don't want anyone else. Just you. I love you."

Sam caught Mikaela in a passionate kiss. "Let's get out of here."

"Let's go home." They smiled at each other.

Epilogue

Written in the Stars by Esmeralda Garnet

ARIES (March 21-April 19) Keep moving in a direction that is sure to bring you pleasure and adventure. Don't sweat the little things. Enjoy the moment. Embrace new people, places and situations. Be perfectly honest.

December twenty-fifth came with a new tradition. Make love before presents are unwrapped. Cook French toast together with a lot of French kisses. Then exchange gifts in front of a crackling fire and a tree sparkling with tinsel. Mikaela unwrapped a new peignoir.

"That's actually for me," Sam said with a laugh.

Then a stunning aquamarine and diamond ring.

"That's for you. It matches your eyes," Sam said.

Sam unwrapped a new tennis racket.

"It's the same racket as mine. I thought you needed an upgrade. Otherwise I'll have an unfair advantage during those strip tennis games."

Sam laughed. "Thank you. It's great."

Mikaela handed Sam a tennis ball canister . . . filled with lacy underthings.

"This may set my game back." He grinned. "But in a good way. I should thank you properly," he said, reaching for her.

"You should," Mikaela said, as she melted into his embrace.

On the way to airport later that afternoon, Mikaela looked over at Sam.

"So maybe now would be a good time to tell you a bit about my parents," Mikaela ventured.

Sam glanced over at her in surprise. "I thought you said your dad was retired and your mom a busy matchmaker."

"Well, that is true . . . sort of."

Sam parked and they headed into the airport terminal. "Which airline?" he asked.

"Actually, that's part of what I wanted to tell you." She led him through the building, through private security, and out onto the tarmac.

Sam didn't say anything, but glanced questioningly at Mikaela.

They were led to a small aircraft with a Palent Enterprises logo. An attendant greeted them at the door. "Welcome aboard, Dr. Finn, sir. Make yourselves comfortable. When you're ready, we've been cleared for takeoff."

"Thank you." Mikaela grasped Sam's hand and pulled him into the cabin. Luxurious seats surrounded a small table. Mikaela guided Sam to the seats and sat down.

"Would you like anything to drink before we take off?" the attendant asked.

"Sam?"

He shook his head, still speechless.

"No. We're fine. Thanks. We're just anxious to get underway."

"Great. If you'll fasten your seatbelts, we'll be off." She disappeared into the rear cabin.

Sam looked at Mikaela. "Something you'd like to tell me?" he asked mildly.

"Well, you know my last name is Finn. That's actually my mother's maiden name. It was easier and well, maybe safer, for me to use that. My dad's surname is actually Palent."

"Palent?"

"Yes, as in Palent Enterprises."

"As in Palent Plastics and Palent Nanophysics and Palent Aeronautics?"

"Well, yes," she admitted reluctantly.

"As in the international, multimillion dollar corporation?"

"It's probably closer to a billion, but yes."

"And you didn't think to tell me the truth about this until now?"

"I told you the truth," she said defensively. "Well, maybe not the whole truth," she admitted sheepishly.

"Anything else you need to tell me?"

"No. That's everything. Except . . . well, to be perfectly honest . . . I love you."

A Note from the Author

To the Reader,

Thank you so much for reading **PERFECTLY HONEST**. Having readers eager for the next installment of a series is the best motivation to create new stories. If you enjoy reading my work as much as I enjoy writing my stories, you might want to:

1) **Sign up for my newsletter.** If you do, you will be notified about the publication date of **PERFECTLY REASONABLE**, the next book in the Perfectly Series. Here's the link: http://www.lindaoconnor.net/contact/

2) **Connect on Facebook, Twitter and my website**. I post excerpts of upcoming releases on my website and my Facebook page as well as announce contests and giveaways.

Visit my website at: http://www.lindaoconnor.net

Follow me on Twitter at: http://www.twitter.com/lindaoconnor98

Like my Author Page on Facebook at:

https://www.facebook.com/pages/Linda-OConnor/229838333874258

3) **Leave a Review**. Please consider writing a review for this book at the e-store where you purchased it. Reviews are very important to authors. They not only help us improve our craft but guide other readers to our books. I would love for you to leave one.

Laugh every day. Love every minute.

Linda O'Connor

CPSIA information can be obtained at www.ICGtesting.com
Printed in the USA
LVOW09s1410010215

425199LV00007B/17/P